"With your sea-green eyes and your hair so fiery, you're definitely a child of daylight, of sunshine," Rob told Cat.

"My goodness, Hepburn!" she exclaimed. "For a scientist, you're waxing astonishingly poetic. And what are you with your black hair and demon eyes—a child of night?"

"Very much so," he said in a voice that suddenly lost its bantering quality. He sounded grim. "From the darkest underbelly of night, as a matter of fact. If you were wise, you'd jump back into that car and escape before it's too late."

Cat blinked. He was serious! She felt a lick of fear. "What on earth do we have in common, Hepburn?"

His eyes made a burning tour of her body. "There's gotta be something..."

Linda Barlow, a former college English teacher, has been writing fiction since she was thirteen. "My first heroine was kidnapped by a pirate," she reports. "Unoriginal, but very romantic!" Between writing, swimming, meditating, and "rather haphazardly keeping house" for her husband and five-year-old daughter, Linda maintains an active interest in psychic phenomena. She and her family make their home in Massachusetts.

Dear Reader:

Before I describe this month's books, I have exciting news. In February 1986, we will introduce a completely new cover design for SECOND CHANCE AT LOVE romances! Everyone at the Berkley Publishing Group is wildly enthusiastic about our new look—a sexy, sophisticated design that is as adult as SECOND CHANCE AT LOVE romances have always been. I'll keep you posted on this important change for SECOND CHANCE AT LOVE ...

In the meantime, this month begins with *Hearts Are Wild* (#298) by new writer Janet Gray, our first romance to star a professional gambler. Emily Farrell is outwardly cool but inwardly vulnerable. Michael Mategna is everything a hero should be—and more! Shattering Emily's calm at the poker table *and* in more private surroundings, he threatens her efforts to win enough money to pay back her father's debts ... and arouses her suspicions about his real motives in pursuing her. A touch of glamour, a hint of intrigue, and a powerful love story make *Hearts Are Wild* a sure bet for any romance lover!

In *Spring Madness* (#299), Aimée Duvall creates another classically wacky romantic comedy by pairing serious-minded radio station owner Kyle Rager with bubbly deejay Meg Randall. When an emergency forces this unlikely twosome to team up on the air, they become an instant hit, an unexpected challenge to their rival station ... and wildly attracted to each other! Nonstop action, zippy dialogue, and outrageous situations all make *Spring Madness* another rollicking roller coaster of a romance from Aimée Duvall.

In *Siren's Song* (#300), ever-popular Linda Barlow creates a powerfully romantic—and deliciously mysterious—world, where everything is not what it seems. When undercover agent Rob Hepburn invades the isolated island home of Cat MacFarlane, he wonders if Cat is really an innocent songstress ... or an accomplice to an international crime ring. Cat wonders if Rob is really an astronomer studying UFO's ... or a dangerous rogue living out an ancient Scot's feud. Unearthly prophecies, haunting melodies, and fast-paced intrigue abound in *Siren's Song*, making it a treat to be savored.

After too long a hiatus, **Katherine Granger** is back with *Man of Her Dreams* (#301), a sparkling, funny romance you're sure to love. Lively, self-reliant Jessie Dillon just can't admit that her gorgeous next-door neighbor, Jake McGuire, is the man she's been searching for all her life. Jake, thank goodness, is definitely *not* a guy to give up easily. Knocking off the competition is no problem—though the process is hilarious—but shutting Jessie up and calming her down long enough to convince her with kisses ... well, that takes some doing! Enjoy!

Employing her unerring instinct for story lines that appeal to romance readers, Dana Daniels has written a compelling story of unrequited love, *Unspoken Longings* (#302). Lesley Evans vows that Joel Easterwood will never know of the secret yearning for him that is tearing her apart. She hides the pain in her heart, and the pain in her hip that resulted from a car accident, with rapier-sharp retorts and a biting wit—never realizing that Joel is equally determined to break through her defenses and bring to life the sensual, giving woman within. *Unspoken Longings* is a deeply moving romance.

In *This Shining Hour* (#303), our second new writer this month, Antonia Tyler, does a terrific job with a challenging combination—a blind hero who's fiercely independent and a warm, giving heroine who's both sensually drawn to him *and* instinctively wants to take care of him. Kent Sawyer is every bit as virile and confident as Eden Fairchild has ever dreamed possible, and he's eager to prove his capabilities at both business ... and pleasure. This rich love story begins as a somewhat deceptively pleasant read, but it soon packs an emotional wallop!

Until next month, happy reading ...

Ellen Edwards

Ellen Edwards, Senior Editor
SECOND CHANCE AT LOVE
The Berkley Publishing Group
200 Madison Avenue
New York, NY 10016

Second Chance at Love

SIREN'S SONG

LINDA BARLOW

SECOND CHANCE AT LOVE
BOOK

Second Chance at Love books are published by
The Berkley Publishing Group
200 Madison Avenue, New York, NY 10016

To my husband, Halûk,
and my daughter, Dilek,
with love

Author's Note

All poems and songs were composed exclusively for this book, with the exception of "Celebration," which I originally wrote (with some minor changes) for my sister Heather's wedding in October 1982.

CHAPTER ONE

"A CASTLE. THE PLACE looks like a medieval castle," Rob Hepburn muttered as he pulled his car into the cobblestone courtyard of Duncan MacFarlane's home on Aberdeen Island. Parking his rented Toyota next to several other cars, he stared up at the imposing edifice before him. Overlooking the rocky Maine coastline, the gray stone structure rose to a height of at least four stories against the clear black sky. With its crenellated archways and the rounded towers at each of the four corners, the only touch of authenticity it lacked was a moat.

Good God. Even though he'd been warned about Duncan MacFarlane's various eccentricities, Rob hadn't expected the old man's home to resemble a highlands fortress. He felt as if he'd stepped through a time warp into fifteenth-century Scotland!

Grimacing, he unfolded his long body from the driver's seat and slammed the car door behind him. Thrusting the keys into his hip pocket, he leaned back briefly against the Toyota. The other cars, he speculated, belonged to MacFarlane's UFO watchers, here tonight for a meeting of the Project Earth Society. Project Earth Society indeed! Rob blew out a harsh breath. He hadn't wanted this blasted assignment in the first place, and he was beginning to like it even less.

Resolutely Rob strode toward the entrance to the outlandish building, the gates of which, he was amused to see, were gaping open. He paused just outside the walls, pricked by the oddest feeling that something was about to happen to him—something he hadn't anticipated in any way. He stood perfectly still, all his senses alert. The premonition was not one of danger, precisely. No, it was more a pleasant sense of expectation. Perhaps it had something to do with the pure, still clarity of the July night, or with the stars that were hanging so gloriously overhead. Or with the music? Faerie music, he thought involuntarily, listening to soft chords on a guitar and a low-toned feminine voice caressing the words of a ballad:

> "My highland love, where art thou roaming?
> Remember, sweet, our nights of loving?
> Oh, come thee soon again?
>
> "Alas, I fear I'll see thee never,
> No more warm whispers in the heather,
> Oh, come thee ne'er again?"

What a lovely voice. Entering the gates, Rob found himself in a large central hall, dimly lit with electric sconces that resembled candles. The inside walls, also gray stone, were covered with colorful handwoven tapestries. A wide stone staircase rose up before him, and archways on either side of him led to the various castle rooms. The music was coming from the left.

Rob moved silently to the archway and peered into a

surprisingly cozy room. There was a fire burning in an enormous hearth, warm Oriental carpets on the floor, and dark wood paneling on the walls. About a dozen people, mostly elderly men and women, were gathered around the fire on sofas and easy chairs, listening to the woman strumming her guitar and singing.

Rob leaned back against the wall, staring at her. She was strikingly beautiful.

The first thing he noticed about her was her hair. The curly brown mane was bright with red highlights that danced in the reflected glimmers of the fire. Surrounded by this wine-dark cloud of flame, her face appeared almost ethereal. Her features were well made: large eyes— he couldn't see the color from this distance—an adorable turned-up nose, a generous mouth. As she sang, her expression was dreamy yet appealingly animated.

Rob's breath came out in a low whistle as he tried to break the spell she had unwittingly cast over him. His eyes drifted over her body, taking advantage of the fact that she hadn't looked in his direction and obviously had no idea he was there.

She was clad in a royal-blue sundress, which left her shoulders, arms, and legs pleasingly bare. Her slender throat was encircled by a thin gold necklace with a locket, the only jewelry she wore. Her dress was just low cut enough to reveal a hint of her sweetly rounded breasts. The guitar hid her midsection, but her legs were long and lithe, with terrific ankles. Her skin was tan and smooth, so smooth, he imagined, that he could almost feel its supple softness beneath his exploring hands . . .

Hold it, Hepburn, he chided himself as his libido clicked into gear. Are you crazy? You don't even know who she is. Besides, you've got a job to do on this island; you're not here to fool around.

But he had no real doubt as to her identity. "Mac-Farlane's got a real knockout of a granddaughter," Cliff Morton, Rob's superior, had told him during his briefing.

This lovely Siren must be she. Rob's gaze shifted slightly to the left, glimpsing for the first time the elderly white-haired man in kilts who was sitting across from the singer. He was strumming his fingers on the arm of his chair in perfect time with the music, and he looked damnably paternal and proud. Duncan MacFarlane, the self-styled "laird" of Aberdeen Island.

Rob's eyes returned to the woman. "Catherine MacFarlane, age twenty-eight, unmarried," Morton had added. "She lives with the old codger—he became her guardian when she was orphaned at the age of twelve. She's a singer-songwriter. Ever heard of the rock group Crusader?"

Rob hadn't.

"I'm not surprised—they're better known abroad than they are here, for some reason. They've toured a lot in Europe and the Far East. We busted one of them, David Kineer, the lead guitarist, a little more than a year ago on possession of marijuana. First offense. He got a suspended sentence. Anyway, Ms. MacFarlane sang for the group until just before the bust. Rumor had it that she and Kineer were an item."

"Possession of marijuana?" Rob had repeated disbelievingly. "And we prosecuted?"

"Actually, Evans, the agent on the case, was after something a lot bigger, but his cover was blown before he could nail Kineer."

"Cocaine? Heroin?"

"No, apart from a little grass, nobody in the group was into drugs. Clean little operation," Morton had said with a sneer. "Evans couldn't prove it, but we think Kineer and his pals were involved in the international weapons trade."

"Ah. I begin to see the connection. And the woman? Was she implicated?"

"Evans insisted she wasn't. She had no idea what

Kineer was really up to. On the other hand"—Morton
had shrugged philosophically—"good though Evans has
always been in his assessment of people, you know what
I always say . . ."

"Never trust a woman," Rob finished grimly. It was
an aphorism upon which he and Morton heartily agreed.

"Right. I had the impression that Evans had a thing
for her himself. No proof, of course, but the lady's a
looker. So you'd better find out whether she still has any
ties to Dave Kineer or anybody else in that crowd. Particularly considering the abandoned airstrip on her grandfather's land."

"You think the gunrunners have been flying the guns
out that way? And that the MacFarlanes may be involved?"

"It's a possibility you'll have to check out."

With this conversation running through his mind, Rob
continued to stare at the auburn-haired singer. He'd expected someone dark and abysmally thin, with circles
under her eyes and a world-weary expression, but instead
she was fair, vibrant, and sweet-faced. And her voice—
it had a lilting quality that was tying his insides in knots.
A *rock* singer? She had a way with a ballad that was
heartbreakingly poignant, moving beyond words. He
closed his eyes, listening.

> "Alas, I fear I'll see thee never,
>   No more warm whispers in the heather,
>   Oh, come thee ne'er again?"

She sings that song as if she's loved and suffered
deeply, he thought vaguely. Pain shivered through him.
He was assailed by an image of Beth.

Ruthlessly he forced the tender memory aside, re-
placing it with other thoughts, other images. Beth was
dead, and as for the women he'd known since, they were

memorable only for their shallowness. Catherine
MacFarlane, very likely, was no different.

Opening his eyes, he indulged in another sweeping
examination of her lithe, slender body. A vivid fantasy
of lustful pursuit and possession rode unbidden through
his mind. He'd been ordered to check her out, hadn't
he? What better way to find out whether she was still
mixed up with her treacherous former lover than to go
after her himself?

Maybe this particular assignment wasn't going to be
so bad, after all.

Just as this idea crossed his mind the ballad wound
down to a close. As the last husky note died the singer
looked up and smiled at her audience, and they all dissolved into delighted applause. Except Rob. He simply
stood there in the archway, willing her to look beyond
the group and acknowledge his presence, his interest, his
attraction. And at last she did. Their eyes met, their gazes
locked, and Rob was seized by one of the most ridiculous
fancies he'd ever indulged—a thought he instantly de-
nied and suppressed: This woman was destined to be his
love.

Cat MacFarlane didn't know who he was or where
he'd come from; she only knew he was there when she
finished singing. Tall, dark, and sexy. As her eyes col-
lided with the intense gaze of the stranger in the archway,
Cat had the oddest sensation of her body falling away
from her soul. She'd seen him before, not in reality, but
in her dreams. He was the demon lover who comes in
the night. And she felt, for one crazy moment, that he
was the one she'd been waiting for all her life.

Cat tossed her head as if to dispel such a highly romantic notion. Romance was something she was staying
away from at present, except in her poetry and songs.
There, in the world of art, the world of illusion, romance

was beautiful, happy, and safe. In the real world, she thought wryly, it could be deceptive and cruel.

Laying aside her guitar, Cat smiled and nodded as her small audience continued to applaud. The stranger, she noted out of the corner of her eye, didn't join in. He was leaning against the cold stone wall, regarding her steadily with a slight smile on his narrow, sensual lips.

Devil.

Amused, both by his stare and by her uncharacteristic reaction to it, she allowed her gaze to slide away from his. She touched the gold locket at her throat—it had belonged to her grandmother, and Cat regarded it as a sort of protective talisman. Who was he? Although people were known to wander casually in and out of her grandfather's weekly meetings of the Project Earth Society, this man didn't look like the type who had come to report a UFO sighting. His posture, his expression, and even the way he was dressed—in a pressed pair of jeans and a dark long-sleeved, tight-collared shirt that made no concession to the humid heat of the balmy July night—suggested a rigid disdain for the group and its subject.

Not that it was easy to take the Project Earth Society seriously. Cat sometimes laughed at them herself, although she didn't entirely discount their claims. She had never seen any of the strange, luminous lights out "over the moors," as Granddad loved to describe the rugged hills of Aberdeen Island, which reminded him so much of his beloved Scotland. But other people had; the close encounters, as all UFO enthusiasts termed them, had been going on for years. There had been a rash of them this summer, and the group had been particularly lively this evening.

"I wonder if you'll see it again tonight," Mrs. Thompson, an elderly widow, said to young Jon Hayden, the lobster fisherman who had reported the most recent spectacular event: a shining globe of white light rising slowly out of the sea not far from his lobster pots. The light had hovered, making soft, beautiful music, Jon had claimed, before streaking off toward the horizon "faster than any jet."

"I'm not so sure I want to see it again," Hayden said uneasily. He and all the others in the group were gathering up their things and heading out through the archway where the stranger stood, giving him no more than a cursory glance. Apparently aliens from space were more interesting than dark, sexy strangers. "I had the weird feeling the thing was checking me out. For all I know, the extraterrestrials were looking for an earthling to kidnap and dissect!"

"Now, now, Jon, there's no need to fear anything like that," Cat's grandfather insisted as he walked out with his guests. Cat half smiled as she found herself silently reciting along with Duncan MacFarlane. She'd heard the bracing speech dozens of times before: "The aliens involved in Project Earth mean no harm to any of us. Down through history they have journeyed to our planet innumerable times, guiding us with their greater insight and intelligence, saving us from destruction. We are their creations, their great experiment. They love us, and we must never fear them."

The little group shuffled out into the cavernous entryway of the old stone castle, leaving Cat alone with the stranger. Still he said nothing—at least not out loud. His electric eyes were saying plenty, though. It was obvious that he thought her grandfather an A-number-one weirdo. Her chin lifted defensively. Her grandfather was a little strange, it was true, and he'd been worse in the two years since her grandmother had died. But Cat adored him and would have defended him against the devil himself, if necessary.

The dark stranger pushed off from the archway to approach her with astonishing grace and smooth physical power. What a hunk, she couldn't help thinking as she rose to her feet. Too bad his handsome face was marred by his obvious impatience and condescension.

He reached her, stopping just short of touching her, a little closer than strict etiquette would have allowed two strangers to stand. "Ms. MacFarlane?" he said in a husky low tone.

Sexy voice, too. Stop drooling, girl, she warned herself. There's bound to be *something* wrong with him. "Yes?"

He was staring at the tendrils of thick hair that fell to her shoulders. "Nice," he said. "I've always loved red hair."

She blinked. "I've always hated it. And I prefer to think of it as auburn." She retreated a step, creating a more conventional distance between them. "Who are you? May I help you in some way?"

"Yes, I believe you can," he said, and he smiled.

His smile was gorgeous, if somewhat restrained. She wondered what it would be like to hear him laugh, a genuine full-bodied laugh. His voice was deep and very musical. And he was tall; she had to tilt her head back slightly to see his face. He was blessed with thick, wavy, dark hair, strong cheekbones, a long blade of a nose, and a severe mouth that nevertheless hinted at sensuality. His eyes were large, brown, and dramatic—eyes you could fall into . . . eyes that would make you fall, were you to be so foolish. They were heavily fringed with dark lashes and arched with delicate brows that might have appeared too feminine had the rest of his features not been so uncompromisingly male.

At a guess, his age was somewhere around thirty-five. His face was faintly lined around the eyes and mouth, and his hair was accented here and there by a hint of gray.

"I want to talk to you," he went on. "You live here with Duncan MacFarlane, your grandfather, right?"

"This is his home, yes," she replied. She was puzzled by the combination of intimacy and formality in his manner. He seemed to feel he had every right to stroll into her home and question her. Was he a police officer or something of that ilk? She tensed automatically at the thought. He hadn't identified himself as such. He hadn't identified himself *at all*. She ran her eyes over his tall, lean form. He looked fit and strong, and he definitely projected authority. But he seemed a little too formal, a little too intellectual, to be a cop.

On the other hand, she remembered wretchedly, Joshua Evans hadn't fit her image of a law enforcement officer, either.

"And his home is his castle," the stranger quipped, waving his hand at the gray stone walls that enclosed them. "I'd been warned, of course, but even so, I could hardly believe my eyes when I pulled up in front of this place. A veritable fortress, complete with turrets and battlements."

"It *is* unusual," she conceded.

He nodded his head at Duncan MacFarlane, who stood in the hallway, saying farewell to his departing guests. "As for him, does he see a psychiatrist? All that junk about flying saucers and benevolent aliens—he sounds deranged."

"He may be eccentric, but he's certainly not deranged," she retorted. "Who are you, anyway? You obviously aren't here because of the Project Earth Society meeting. Why have you come barging into our home?"

"Actually, I *am* here because of the Project Earth Society meeting." His tone was similar to one Cat might have used to refer to a meeting of the Ku Klux Klan. "My name's Rob Hepburn. I'm a scientist, a government astronomer." He paused for an instant, regarding her with narrowed eyes, almost as if he were daring her to contradict him. "I'm staying out at the Aberdeen Observatory," he added, referring to Aberdeen Island's pride

and joy—the small observatory with the sixty-inch re-
flecting telescope. "I'm here to investigate the so-called
UFO sightings on Aberdeen Island."

"Oh, no!" Cat cried. All sorts of unpleasant ramifi-
cations instantly rose up in her imagination. "You're not
going to tell that to my grandfather, I hope."

"Of course I am. I have some questions I want to ask
him—that's the reason I'm here tonight." Rob was annoyed at himself for the slight hesitation in stating his
cover story. He rarely made slips like that, but there was
something disturbing about looking into those huge eyes
of hers—they were as green as the sea, he could see
now—and lying. Still, he reminded himself, it wasn't
exactly a lie. He *was* here to investigate the sightings,
even though he was ninety-nine percent certain they were
gun smugglers, not UFO's. And he *was* an astronomer.
At least he had been, many years ago.

"I assure you, in almost all these close encounter
cases, the unidentifiable flying objects prove to be iden-
tifiable, after all," he went on. "The average idiot, it's
true, might take a weather balloon for a flying saucer,
or a jumbo jet with its landing lights on for a meteorite
about to decimate some major city, but no scientist would
ever make such a mistake."

"Maybe so, but the very last thing the Project Earth
Society wants to hear is that the UFO's are weather bal-
loons! It would destroy their most cherished illusion."
Cat lifted her chin, wondering if there was any way to
dissuade him from pursuing his investigation. The people
of Aberdeen Island were proud of their "extraterrestrials." It would break their hearts—her grandfather's in
particular—if the mysterious spacecraft were proven to
be some sort of natural phenomena. "I don't like people
who destroy illusions, Mr. Hepburn." Once again she
had a fleeting image of Josh. "It's cruel and unnecessary."

"I disagree. It's the illusions themselves that are cruel.
People should learn to accept the world as it is, with all

its sundry imperfections. It takes a certain amount of courage to face reality, that's certainly true. But I don't have much respect for those weak-minded souls who view life through a veil of false illusions."

"What a stoical philosophy," she mocked softly. "Not to mention condescending and cynical, too."

Hepburn's expression hardened. He reached into the back pocket of his jeans and drew out a newspaper clipping. "All right, Ms. MacFarlane, listen to this: 'Aeons ago, long before the annals of recorded time, the planet Earth was colonized by aliens. We are a test-tube society, according to Duncan MacFarlane of Aberdeen Island. Men and women were brought to Earth from another galaxy, to see whether we would thrive and develop.'" He raised his eyes. "Now really, Ms. MacFarlane, this is a bit far out, even for a flying saucer enthusiast. Does your grandfather seriously believe this nonsense?"

"Well, uh, yes," Cat admitted. She felt a little ridiculous. Although she didn't subscribe to her grandfather's theories, she certainly wasn't going to mock them. "We were put here, supposedly, with barely the wherewithal to survive, to see if we could band together and learn to cope with a relatively hostile environment."

"Sounds pretty sadistic."

"Not really. We weren't abandoned, you see. The extraterrestrials responsible for Project Earth return periodically to help us if we're in danger of extinction. It's not really a new idea. You know, I presume, about the ancient evidence for visitors from another planet? The creatures in space helmets etched on the walls of the cavemen's dwellings, for example? The ancient landing strips on the Plain of Nasca in Peru?"

He raised his dark eyebrows. "Don't forget Atlantis, Stonehenge, and the Great Pyramid."

She smiled spontaneously. "I'm not. They're all mysteries, aren't they, that your science has yet to explain."

"Good God! You look like a sensible woman. How

can you stand there and discuss this with a straight face?"

She tilted her head to one side as she considered him. From what she'd read about government scientists who investigated UFO reports, he fit the type exactly: skeptical, rational, and condescending. Why was it, she wondered, that members of the scientific community were so quick to dismiss anything they couldn't see, feel, hear, and measure? Although she herself wasn't a confirmed believer in visitors from other planets, she believed that *some* UFO's, at least, were of mysterious origin. In fact, many of the "explanations" dreamed up by various Air Force and federal investigators were even more wildly improbable than the phenomena themselves.

"'There are more things on heaven and earth, Horatio, than are dreamt of in your philosophy,'" she quoted gently.

"Come on," he retorted. "If your grandfather had his way, he'd redraw the Bermuda Triangle to include Aberdeen Island."

He sounded so outraged at the idea that Cat couldn't restrain an impulse to laugh. Her mirth merely escalated when he glared at her in response. His deep brown eyes fixed on her in annoyance, but as she continued to grin at him, they abruptly changed, becoming at once softer and more intense. He was staring at her mouth. She licked her lips a little nervously and touched her necklace. When he raised his eyes to meet hers, she could sense his thought as if it were her own—this devilishly handsome man was fantasizing about what it would be like to touch her, taste her, brush his lips over her own.

Uh-oh. Cat felt the unmistakable rush of heightened sensual awareness. Her lips began to tingle as if he had already kissed them. My God, what I am thinking of? she asked herself. He was attractive, yes, and there definitely seemed to be some kind of chemistry working there. Or was she imagining it? She sincerely hoped so! She'd done very well for the past year. She was over Josh, over romance, over sensual entanglements of any kind. She was off men, temporarily at least. And no black-haired, sexy-eyed demon was going to change her mind about that!

"There's no point in arguing. I somehow doubt that you and I will ever see eye-to-eye on the matter," she said, half expecting him to take offense at her tone, which was as sarcastic as she, normally a good-natured and friendly person, could make it. But Hepburn didn't seem to notice. And they were definitely not seeing eye-to-eye. *His* eyes were staring at her breasts, which were unconfined beneath the royal-blue cotton of her sundress.

The corners of her mouth turned up. "What's the matter, astronomer? Has a supernova suddenly sprouted in the middle of my chest?"

He raised his gaze to her face and smiled ruefully. She thought she could detect a faint flush rising over his cheekbones, and that surprised her. "I'm sorry. I didn't mean to be so obvious." He paused a moment, then added, "You're very pretty."

His straightforward manner floored her. For some reason it didn't come out sounding like a line; his face, his eyes, his voice all *seemed* totally sincere.

"Thank you," she said a little unsteadily. She cleared her throat. "You have yet to explain exactly why you've come here tonight, Mr. Hepburn."

"I told you, I have some questions for your grandfather. And a few for you, too," he added. He gave her another tight smile. When he smiled, the demonic quality about him dissipated slightly, but not enough. To get rid of it entirely, he would have to be lured into laughter. How difficult would it be, she wondered, to get the devil to laugh? "By the way," he added, "please call me Rob."

She smiled agreeably even as she warned herself that this handsome but intolerant man was merely turning on the sexual charm. For some reason, though, the warning wasn't taking. It had been a long time since she'd responded so easily and naturally to anyone's come-hither signals. Not since Josh.

"My grandfather will be back any moment," she said. "I'll introduce you, but I'd be grateful if you didn't plunge right in and tell him that you've come to debunk the Project Earth Society. *You* might be unsympathetic to other people's illusions, but I will do my best to protect his."

His smile disappeared. "I'm certain there are no UFO's on this island. But naturally I have to check out all the reports, and your grandfather is the self-proclaimed expert on the subject. His illusions don't concern me; I'm here to get at the truth."

"Whatever questions you have, you can ask me," she said quickly, forgetting everything else in her determination to protect her grandfather. "I know just as much about the phenomena as he does. Please, Rob. Don't ruin his evening." Unconsciously she leaned closer to him, reaching out to place her hand on his arm. She could feel hard muscles beneath her fingertips; they flexed slightly in response to her touch, and her own breath came hard. She snatched her hand away, hoping he wouldn't take her unthinking gesture as a come-on.

But it seemed he did. He was smiling again, but there was something predatory now about those curving lips, those hot brown eyes. "You know the details of the sightings—days, times, descriptions of the duration, and movements of the lights?"

"Yes. We've kept records. I have access to them."

"I'll require a guided tour of the island. I want to check out all the areas where the UFO's have supposedly hovered or landed."

"I'm the obvious choice for that," she said reluctantly. "Granddad's not spry enough anymore to be chasing all over this rough terrain. And I know the spots, even the most secret ones. After Granddad, I'm the nearest thing to an expert on the subject."

His eyes brushed over her—her throat, her breasts, her hips, her legs were all exposed to his slow, considering stare. "In that case, I suggest we make a deal, Catherine." There was something very enticing about the way he said her name. "You be my source of information, and I leave your grandfather alone. What do you say to that?"

What could she say? Taking it as casually as possible seemed the only sensible thing to do. "Fine with me, astronomer," she said, affecting a shrug.

"I'd like to get started as soon as possible, if you don't mind. Tomorrow. We could go out together, and you could"—he paused for an instant, his eyes on her lips once again—"show me all your secret spots."

Cat flushed. What did he think she was offering, for heaven's sake? If his price for keeping her grandfather in the dark was *that* high, she wasn't prepared to pay it!

"I think we ought to get one thing straight, Mr. Hepburn," she said severely. "You're a rationalistic scientist who believes everything in the world can be explained and quantified. I'm an artist who creates music and poetry out of the very illusions you despise. We have nothing in common, and any interaction between us will have to be *strictly* business."

He raised his finely drawn eyebrows in a half-amused, half-alluring gesture that was as old as the game that had inexplicably sprung up between them. "There's one poetic saying that even the most rationalistic of us adhere to," he said softly. "Nothing ventured, nothing gained."

She was not mollified. "Well, kindly keep your venturing to the matter at hand: UFO's and close encounters!"

She regretted the slip as soon as it passed her lips, and, devil that he was, he didn't hesitate to pounce. "A close encounter was exactly what I had in mind," he said, and he took a step toward her.

CHAPTER TWO

CAT BACKED AWAY from the sensual threat, but Rob Hepburn followed her, looking as if he had every intention of initiating a close encounter right there in front of the flickering fire. Surely he wasn't going to kiss her? Not if she had any say in the matter! "What do you think you're doing?" She made her voice as scathingly frosty as possible. "For heaven's sake, Rob, we've only just met."

The look in those deep brown eyes was heated but playful, the first real indication that the man might have a sense of humor. A rather *odd* sense of humor, perhaps, but ... "I have a feeling we're going to get to know each other fast," he drawled.

His voice, his eyes, and his body were close—too close. Good grief! She retreated another step. There was an ominous quaking in the pit of her stomach that spoke eloquently of the man's unprecedented power over her. Why did he have to be so attractive, blast it all?

"You're very confident, aren't you?" she retorted. "Do you always come on so strong within ten minutes of meeting a woman?"

"I haven't touched you yet," he pointed out. The *yet* seemed to hang in the air between them, both a promise and a threat.

"Some women may enjoy the old caveman approach, but I assure you, it doesn't appeal to me!"

"I'm sorry." He shrugged somewhat ruefully, then grinned. "There's a full moon out tonight, so I guess I'm just not responsible for my behavior."

Cat felt herself begin to relax, even though she was still very much aware of the waves of attraction flowing between them. "Leave it to an astronomer to come up with that as an excuse."

"Clever, huh?"

"But hardly very scientific or rational. Deep down, Mr. Hepburn, you're as superstitious as anybody else."

Before he could reply to this, they were interrupted by her grandfather's booming voice. "Well, young man, who are you, and what deviltry are you whispering in my bonnie granddaughter's ear?"

Rob turned sharply as Duncan MacFarlane entered the room. Cat took the opportunity to inch away from Rob. Dressed in his traditional kilts, Duncan MacFarlane stalked toward them like a lion coming to safeguard its young. He was a big man, tall and hearty, even at his advanced age of seventy-five. Indeed, with his white hair, thick as a lion's mane, there was something distinctly leonine about Granddad, Cat noted proudly. Something fierce and rather noble.

Cat nudged Rob in the ribs with one elbow. "You're not going to tell him why you're here," she reminded him in a whisper. "I'll not have him upset."

Hoping he would honor their agreement despite her obvious rejection of his advances, she hastened to make the introductions. "Granddad, this is Rob. He's a newcomer to the island, an astronomer. He'll be, uh, working over at the observatory with Emma for a couple of weeks. Rob, this is my grandfather, Duncan MacFarlane."

MacFarlane smiled genially and held out his hand. "An astronomer, you say? Excellent. Emma St. Charles, our resident astronomer at the Aberdeen Observatory, is a good friend of ours. We'll all have to get together and have a good long talk."

"Fine. There are several things I'd like to discuss with you," Rob said smoothly.

Cat winced, but thank goodness he left it at that.

"Anytime, lad, anytime. We welcome everybody here. Aberdeen Island's a very friendly place, you'll find. What did you say your name was? Rob? Short for Robert? A good Scots name, that."

"Robert Hepburn. And my family did come from Scotland, I believe several generations ago."

There was a moment's silence; then Duncan MacFarlane's expression altered completely. "Robert *Hepburn?*" he repeated, his blue eyes glinting ominously. "Are you telling me there's a Hepburn here, in my castle, chatting up my granddaughter? I won't have it!"

"Granddad, what on earth are you talking about?" Cat demanded, astonished. Rob's face had also changed, she noted. His pleasant features were rearranging themselves into a sneer.

Duncan MacFarlane raised his arm and pointed to the archway. "Out, you spawn of the devil! A Hepburn! Good God, I'll have no Hepburns here!"

"Grandfather!" Cat cried, appalled. She'd never heard Duncan MacFarlane raise his voice in anger to a guest. "How can you be so rude?"

"You stay out of this, woman!" Granddad shouted. He strode over to the fireplace and yanked his old-fashioned ceremonial sword down from the wooden rack where it was so proudly mounted. While Cat stared in dismay, her grandfather raised the sword on high and brandished it at Rob. The astronomer shot Cat a quick look that seemed to say, *See? I told you he was deranged.*

"The Hepburns are a cursed breed," Duncan Mac-Farlane ranted. "Your great-great-grandfather was murdered by a Hepburn, Catherine—and that was only the most recent of their crimes against our clan. They're a vicious lot. For generations there's been a blood feud between the Hepburns and the MacFarlanes."

"My God, this is the twentieth century! We left clan warfare and all that sort of craziness back in Scotland."

Her grandfather ignored her. "I warn you," he continued to address Rob, "if you don't want to feel my blade in your gut, you thieving, murdering blackguard, you'll leave my castle and never set foot on my property again!"

"I'll leave for now, you balmy old bastard," Rob retorted. His color, too, was high. "But I'll be back, I promise you. We have a number of matters to discuss, you and I." He turned to Cat. "Come outside with me. I have something to say to you."

Cat wasn't crazy about Rob's tone, but her grandfather liked it even less. "She's not going anywhere with you. Not now, not ever. I know the way you Hepburns deal with women—vile rogues and seducers, all of you. You have that rakish look about you, twentieth century or no!"

"Grandfather!" Cat was worried now. Duncan MacFarlane was almost as obsessed with Scottish history as he was with UFO's, but he'd never pulled anything like this. Maybe a psychiatrist was in order after all? "You'd better go, Rob. I don't know what the matter is, but I think it would be best if you left quickly. I'll talk to you tomorrow."

Her grandfather whirled on her. "You'll do no such thing, Catherine!" he roared. "You'll *never* talk to him, do you hear me? I absolutely forbid it!" He snapped his attention back to Rob. "And as for you, if you touch my

granddaughter, Hepburn, I'll have your head on the battlements."

All at once Cat found herself beating down a strong
urge to laugh. Really, it was too ridiculous! She was
twenty-eight years old, and her grandfather was ready to
kill a man for admiring her.

Lighten up, she wanted to say to both of them, but
the age-old masculine lines had already been drawn. Her
grandfather was behaving abominably, but Rob was proving just as capable of aggressive machismo.

"My head on the battlements, huh?" he drawled.
"There's no way I'm going to be able to resist a challenge
like that."

With one long stride he reached Cat's side and jerked
her into his arms. "You're well beyond the age of consent,
lovely lady," he muttered just before his head came down.
He held her close, ravaging her mouth with a kiss that
made her head spin. Her mouth opened traitorously under
his, and for a moment she felt the erotic sliding of his
tongue.

He drew back, leaving her lips hot and damp and
achingly aroused. "Tomorrow," he whispered as her
grandfather raised his sword over his head and let out a
bloodcurdling war cry. Rob released her just as swiftly
as he'd seized her, and, tossing her a farewell grin, he
ran across the chamber and disappeared into the night.

It took Cat more than an hour to get her grandfather—
not to mention herself—settled down and into bed that
night. Duncan MacFarlane insisted on dragging her into
the study, where he kept his notes on Scottish clan history,
which was the only other subject besides UFO's that held
any real interest for him.

"Read this," he insisted, thrusting some yellowing
pamphlets into her hand. "Then you'll understand."

There really had been a feud between the MacFarlanes
and the Hepburns, Cat discovered. It had started back in

the fifteenth century when Patrick Hepburn kidnapped
Enoch MacFarlane's daughter, Mary, a sweet young
woman who had planned to enter a convent and dedicate
her life to God. Seduced and abandoned by the heartless
Hepburn, Mary MacFarlane had slowly wasted away and
died, calling upon her kinsmen to avenge her.

The MacFarlanes, apparently, had proceeded to do
just that, and from then on it was the usual sort of thing—
pillaged castles, rapes, and bloodshed. The Hepburns
had started the feud, her grandfather insisted, but it
sounded to Cat as if both families had done their share
of violence. She indignantly informed her grandfather
that she couldn't dredge up much sympathy for either
side.

Cat was in bed, attempting to unwind from the heady
excitement of the evening, when the phone on her night
table rang. She grabbed it on the first ring, anxious that
her grandfather not be disturbed.

"Hello?"

"Catherine?"

Cat felt a little curl of sensation in the pit of her
stomach as she recognized the deep, pleasant voice of
Rob Hepburn.

"This is your mortal enemy," he said. "Are you going
to come out with me tomorrow of your own free will,
or do I have to lay siege to the castle and snatch you
away on horseback?"

"I think I'd rather enjoy being snatched, just to see
how it felt to live in those melodramatic times," she said
lightly. "But Granddad would probably have a stroke."

"*I* nearly had a stroke when he came at me with that
broadsword."

"You shouldn't have kissed me like that—it was a
deliberate act of provocation."

"I lost my head." His voice turned husky as he added,
"But I'd do it again. The rewards far outweigh the risks."

Cat shifted fretfully in bed as she remembered the

warmth of his hard mouth lingering on hers. "Are you
flirting with me, Hepburn? I ought to hang up on you,
now that I know the men in your clan are all vile rogues
and seducers. It was a Hepburn, you know, who kidnapped Mary Queen of Scots and forced her to wed him."

"It was?"

"Yes, indeed. She lost the throne as a result. She had
to abdicate in favor of her son."

"She abdicated? I thought they chopped off her head."

"That was years later, in England. You don't know
your Scottish history very well, do you?"

"No," he conceded. "I was born in this country, as
were my parents and my grandparents. I've never given
my heritage much thought. Was there really a clan feud
between your family and mine, or did your grandfather
make the whole thing up?"

"The feud's real enough, it seems. Granddad showed
me some historical accounts of the lamentable behavior
of both families. The Hepburns had a distinct propensity
for seducing and abandoning the MacFarlane women."

"Yeah?" He was clearly fascinated with the possibilities. "But that was in the old days. You're not going to
hold the sins of our forefathers against me, are you,
Catherine?"

"No," she laughed. "Unlike my grandfather, I'm not
living in the past."

He chuckled, sending new scurryings of sensation
through Cat. Her response to him continued to surprise
her. When he'd been hovering so closely over her, her
attraction to his tall, lean body was understandable; but
here she was, nowhere near the man, getting hot flashes
from a disembodied voice.

You'd better watch your step, Cat warned herself, or
all the pleasures of a safe, uninvolved, man-free existence are going to go flying out the window.

"You know, it's funny," he went on. "With his interest
in UFO's, I thought it was the future your grandfather

was obsessed with, not the Dark Ages. Isn't there something incongruous about living in a castle and believing in E.T.?"

"Not really. One of Granddad's theories is that time doesn't exist, that it's an illusion. According to him, we may have difficulty perceiving it, but everything is really happening simultaneously in a sort of continuous present. Clan feuds and modern technology, warriors on horseback and starships streaking away into the night are all current events to Granddad. 'As it was in the beginning, is now and ever shall be,' in other words."

"That's irrational," he said indignantly. "We can prove time exists. The time dimension, in fact, is crucial to astronomers; we measure distance by it, and all our calculations depend upon it. If time is an illusion, so is the universe."

"Well, of course, that's true, too." She smiled into the receiver, delighting in this opportunity to tease him. "The universe *is* an illusion. Beautiful, as so many illusions are, but illusory nonetheless."

"You're as crazy as he is if you believe that."

"Not crazy, just philosophical. There's nothing new about the idea. Was Plato crazy?"

"Probably," he said uncompromisingly. "He certainly didn't understand the scientific method. We've come a long way since the superstitious days of ancient Greece—you'll have to admit that."

"Have we? I wonder."

"Catherine . . ." His voice assumed a lower timbre. "This is all very interesting, but I didn't call you to discuss philosophy. Or science, for that matter. What about tomorrow? I want to see you, bloodthirsty grandfather or not."

"You heard him; I've been forbidden your company."

"You mean you're going to be ruled by that?" He seemed not to have heard the playful note in her voice. "Do you allow him to interfere in your personal life?"

"No, not really. I've no wish to hurt him, though. He's an old man who's set in his ways, but I love him very much. Forgive me, but I hardly know *you*." She paused, then added, "And as for my personal life, I thought all you wanted was for me to answer your questions about the UFO's." This was a lie—she knew without a flicker of doubt that he wanted more from her than that, but it didn't seem particularly strategic to admit it. "Once we take care of that piece of business, our association will come to an end."

There was silence on the line for an instant or two; then Rob said, "Cat? Is there someone else in your life? If so, please tell me now."

She was astonished both by the intensity of the question and by the palpable impatience with which he seemed to await her answer. "There's no one," she admitted. "There was somebody about a year ago, but that's over now."

"What happened?"

"We broke up."

"Why?"

"Look, Rob, what has this got to do with anything?" She was damned if she was going to answer questions about Josh; even thinking about him brought back a slew of unruly emotions. Oh, she was over it now—she'd told Rob the truth about that—but some bitterness remained and probably always would. She certainly didn't care to be reminded of the way she'd been duped and manipulated by the man she had fallen so hard for, the man who had lied to her and deceived her.

Until her unfortunate experience with Josh Evans, Cat had always believed herself to be a fairly good judge of people. How wrong he had proved her! In the cruelest way imaginable, Josh had taught her not only that she couldn't trust him, but that she couldn't even trust herself. "I'm not involved with anybody, and I don't intend to be. I'm taking a sabbatical," she added, "from men."

"A sabbatical?" he repeated wryly. "What is this, the New Celibacy or something?" Rob's tone hardened. "This guy from a year ago—did he do something to put you off the sex as a whole?"

Again she was taken aback by the demand in his tone. He seemed to think he had a *right* to question her. Well, two could play that game. "What about you?" she asked. "You're not in a relationship at present, I presume?" An afterthought came to her. "Or married?"

"I was married once. My wife died."

"I'm sorry," she hastened to say. "Was it recently?"

"No." His voice clipped the subject off. "It was a long time ago. But we can tell each other our life stories some other time. Right now I'm more interested in having you show me around the island." He paused. "We had a deal. I kept my part."

Well, she thought, at least she'd learned how to cut off personal questions: Just shoot them back at him. "So you did," she said briskly. "I'd better meet you somewhere, though. I don't think it would be a very good idea for you to show up at the castle."

"Meet me here at the observatory."

"Fine. What time?"

"If you come around noon, we could take along a picnic lunch."

"All right. Shall I pack some sandwiches?"

"Leave that to me. I'll provide the food; you can provide the, uh, entertainment."

"What does *that* mean?" she demanded suspiciously. "Listen, you, maybe I should pay more attention to my grandfather's warnings and take care not to be alone with the descendant of a villainous Scottish clan."

"Don't worry," he chuckled. "Unlike my violent forebears, I don't mean to carry you off and ravish you. At least, I thought we'd get to know each other first."

"That's very reassuring! You'll get to know me and *then* you'll ravish me?"

"Only if you're willing," he said softly, his voice a deep caress.

Cat's breath came faster and faster. She couldn't deny it: The man was irresistibly sexy. She was going to have to be careful, or this relationship could escalate swiftly out of control. "Good night, Hepburn," she murmured. "See you tomorrow."

"Dream of me," he suggested as he hung up.

To her chagrin she settled down in bed and proceeded to do exactly that.

On the ground floor apartment of the Aberdeen Observatory where he was camping out, Rob lay back on the sofa bed and ran the conversation over in his mind. He smiled, pleased that he'd convinced Cat to keep their date tomorrow despite the objections of her balmy old grandfather. But . . . his smile faded as he admitted there was something about this situation that bothered him. He didn't like lying to this woman.

Usually he didn't give it a thought—lying about his profession was one of the givens of working undercover. But this time, for some reason, he hated the deception. He would have liked to face Catherine MacFarlane honestly and openly, without games, without deceit. He would have liked to be himself.

Damn the job! He was getting too old for this sort of thing. It had been stimulating in the beginning when, gut-tearingly angry over Beth's death, he had chucked his position as a junior astronomer and taken his diplomat father's advice about applying for an Agency job. The work had had all the action and violence he'd probably needed at the time to achieve catharsis, but did he need it any longer? Did he *want* it? Beth was dead; he'd accepted that. Arresting all the bad guys on the face of the earth wasn't going to bring her back.

Like so many other jobs, this one had lost its appeal. He'd seen too much of what was grimmest in human nature: greed, betrayal, disloyalty, hatred. Sometimes he wondered whether there were any genuinely honest, decent people left in the world. As an astronomer he'd confronted the vast darkness of the night sky, but he'd been spared any knowledge of the darkness in people's souls. Now he was intimate with evil, and he was afraid, sometimes, that it might be rubbing off on him.

With all the discipline he'd worked so hard to acquire, Rob forced such thoughts out of his mind. They weren't helpful, he'd learned. It was no good to brood about matters he couldn't control. Matters he *could* control, on the other hand . . . He thought once again of Catherine.

It had been a long time since he'd been so strongly drawn to a woman. Besides being desirable as hell, she was pleasant and easy to talk to. Once again he seemed to hear her light, husky laugh. Her singing voice was magical, and her voice on the telephone was equally bewitching.

Putting his hands behind his head and stretching his long legs out as far as he could on the short sofa bed, Rob relived the delightful feel of Cat MacFarlane's lips shivering under his. Her breath was warm and fragrant, and her mouth had opened to him as readily as if they'd kissed a thousand times. He tried to recall how the rest of her body had felt, but there hadn't been enough time to form an impression. How close had he held her during that brief, impetuous embrace? Had they touched chest to breast, thigh to thigh? If so, why couldn't he recreate the feeling? Her mouth was all he remembered, dammit. He'd been totally swept up by a kiss.

Next time, he swore, he'd pay more attention to what he was doing. He'd slide his hands over her breasts, caressing the tips until they budded with excitement. He'd smooth his palms along her sides, around her waist, and down. He'd urge her hips into the cradle of his, letting her feel how much she aroused him. Did he have the same effect on her? Probably not, he sighed, his mouth twisting with self-derision as he tried to put a rein on his erotic imaginings. Just because he'd gone off the deep end within moments of meeting her didn't mean she felt anything similar. She'd accused him of caveman tactics, after all.

He'd once read somewhere that a man usually knew within six seconds of meeting a woman whether or not he wanted to make love to her. Women—even the shallow-hearted, empty-souled women he tended to meet in his line of work—were slower to make up their minds. Six hours, maybe, six days. Six *weeks*. He groaned at the thought. Catherine MacFarlane wasn't empty souled, and he doubted that she was particularly easy bodied. He couldn't wait six weeks for her—he didn't have six weeks. Morton wanted him to wrap up this assignment in under two.

Morton. Dammit. Grimly Rob reminded himself that he was not on this island for the pursuit of sensual pleasure, but to investigate the possibilities that the "UFO's" were in fact airplanes, smuggling weapons out of the United States to illegal purchasers abroad. Worse, the old airstrip that he and Morton believed to be the landing place of the gunrunners was located somewhere on Duncan MacFarlane's property. What if the old madman was not only obsessed by but responsible for the so-called UFO's? And what if the lovely songstress Catherine, the known associate of a suspected smuggler, was his accomplice?

As much as he hated to face the possibility, particularly now that he'd met her—kissed her—Cat MacFarlane was a suspect in this case. She had known and perhaps loved David Kineer. Evans, the previous agent on the case, had believed her innocent, and Rob certainly hoped it was true. But if she wasn't . . . The muscles in Rob's jaw set in a mask of harsh determination. If she wasn't, he would personally rout the MacFarlane clan just as thoroughly as the Hepburns had reportedly done in the past.

CHAPTER THREE

A WARM SEA BREEZE tossed Cat's hair as she drove up the steep mountain road that led to the Aberdeen Observatory the next day at noon. She had the sunroof open on her Honda Accord, for it was a hot summer day. The sky was so blue it dazzled her eyes. And the ocean, which billowed out at the foot of the rocky cliffs below the observatory—how wild and inviting it looked! If she hadn't known from years of experience how numbing the water was, even on these sultry July days, she might have been tempted to fling off her shirt and cutoffs and dive from the cliffs to cavort in its depths like a dolphin.

"Isn't it torture?" she said to Rob Hepburn when she pulled to a stop in front of the white stone observatory. He was outside waiting for her as she drove up, leaning against the open hood of an old car and looking bone-tinglingly sexy in a pair of jeans and *no* shirt. His sun-bronzed torso was lean and subtly muscled. His chest was lightly dusted with black ringlets that matched the hair on his head. His jeans were so snug they ought to be illegal.

"Isn't what torture?" he drawled, coming right over and leaning on the car door, his face only inches from her own. By daylight his eyes were a deep, earthy brown . . . and every bit as magnetic as they'd seemed last night. They were underscored by a network of fine lines, and there was also a tiny furrow in his brow that hadn't been so noticeable in the dim light. She could smell his faint scent, tangy and masculine. Was it cologne or the natural perfume of his skin? Whichever it was, she liked it.

She waved her hand at the sea. "That. Doesn't it look tempting? Doesn't it make you want to hold your breath and jump in without a thought for the consequences?"

"Yeah," he said huskily. Instead of wasting a glance on the ocean, his eyes dropped to her breasts. She knew the yellow cambric blouse she was wearing over her denim cutoffs was not particularly seductive, but he still made her feel undressed. "Very tempting," he agreed. "I want to jump in, all right. The sooner the better."

Self-consciously she shut off the engine and got out of the car. "I was referring to the Atlantic Ocean."

"So was I," he said, grinning so winningly that she couldn't stop herself from smiling back. His smile was no longer condescending or tight. His smile, in fact, was devastating. "But I've been warned I'll freeze my bal— er, certain portions of my anatomy—if I give in to any such reckless temptations."

Cat swallowed, then decided against making any further remarks along these treacherous lines. Why did he have to look like something out of a Calvin Klein jeans ad, dammit? He was a troublemaker, she reminded herself, out to undermine her grandfather's harmless fantasies about benevolent aliens from other planets. And he was a Hepburn to boot!

"Are you ready?" She looked from the car he'd been tinkering with to his strong bare chest. "We can take my car if there's something wrong with yours. You'll get sunburned like that, you know."

"Think so?" He glanced down at his own body as if he'd never seen it before, then nodded and said, "I'll pull on a shirt. I was fiddling with Emma's wreck, trying to get the old thing running—that's why I'm dressed like this."

That was nice. The helpful type. Solicitous of old ladies and their crotchety cars.

"Mine's parked around the back," he continued. "You're early, you know."

"Am I? Sorry—I never wear a watch."

"Naturally. Someone who believes time is an illusion is not going to be troubled by anything as mechanical as a watch."

She laughed, noting that his left wrist sported an elaborate timepiece that probably did everything from waking him up in the morning to making his coffee. "I believe in natural timing," she told him, glancing overhead at the sun. "The sun's high in the sky, so it must be noon."

"Nature lady, huh? You know, I believe you. With your sea-green eyes and your hair so fiery, you're definitely a child of daylight, of sunshine."

"My goodness, Hepburn! For a scientist, you're waxing astonishingly poetic. And what are you with your black hair and demon eyes—a child of night?"

"Very much so," he said in a voice that suddenly lost its bantering quality. He sounded grim. "From the darkest underbelly of night, as a matter of fact. If you were wise, you'd jump back into that car and escape before it's too late."

Cat blinked. He was serious! For an instant something darkly intense was communicated to her, a brief glimpse of dangerous, roiling emotion. She felt a lick of fear. There was a great deal more to this man than was evident on the surface. She sensed pain lurking in him and potential hurt looming just ahead for her.

Wonderful. That was all she needed. When, troubled, she didn't respond, the look in Rob's eyes gentled. His expression loosened once again into a grin, and whatever it was that had flashed so vividly disappeared. "Don't worry, sun-child," he said, reaching out to tousle her hair as if she were a kid, "I'm exaggerating."

"Hmm, I don't know." Her fingers caught the gold locket and worried it. "What on earth do we have in common, Hepburn?"

His eyes did their burning tour of her body again. "There's gotta be something."

"There's that," she acknowledged. She looked candidly into those expressive brown eyes. "But it's not enough for me, Rob."

"No?"

"No." Her voice was very firm.

He blew out a breath. "I wish I could pretend not to know what we're talking about." He leaned closer. "Cat. I've been looking forward to this all morning. All night, in fact. I tossed and turned in bed, hardly sleeping at all. Don't tell me again that you're taking a sabbatical from men. Don't even hint that I haven't got a whistle of a chance. You don't want a despairing astronomer on your hands all day, do you?"

"Rob, we just met!"

"Sometimes it happens like that."

"Not to me."

"Are you sure? I knew the moment I saw you that I wanted to make love to you, Catherine." His eyes had taken on a slumberous expression that was outrageously seductive. She felt hypnotized, mesmerized. She remembered how he'd appeared out of nowhere last night, a demon conjured up by some strange erotic powers of darkness.

"No, I knew it even *before* I saw you," he amended. "I knew from the moment I heard your voice. You drew me into the castle the way the Sirens lured the sailors of old to their deaths on the rocks. I listened and was lost."

"I'm considering taking your advice about jumping into the car and escaping, Hepburn," she said dryly. "I used to sing professionally, and believe me, I've heard the old Siren line before."

She thought she caught a glimpse of vulnerability in his eyes before he quickly hid it. "Well, I guess that's two strikes against me," he said after a split second's pause. "The caveman didn't work, and now the impassioned plea bites the dust. I'd better be real careful about what I try next."

She felt a flutter of regret. She hadn't meant to hurt his feelings. "I'm sorry. I didn't mean to—"

"No problem," he interrupted. "Next time just say, 'Down, boy,' and I'll get the message faster, I promise." He turned back toward the observatory, sending a frisson of apprehension through her. She felt numb as she watched him lope up the steps to the front door of the domed building. Was he deserting her? Damn! He couldn't be that touchy, could he?

"I'll be right back with the picnic basket," he called over his shoulder, to her immense relief. "Want to come inside? Have you seen the place before?"

"Uh, yes, lots of times. Emma's a good friend of ours. Where is she today, down at her cottage?"

"Yeah, sleeping, no doubt. The hours are brutal— working all night the way she has to."

"And you're camping out inside while you're here?"

"That's right. It's not the Ritz, but it's home." He disappeared inside the doorway. Cat knew there was a one-room apartment there, with a kitchenette, a sofa bed, and a few others sticks of furniture. Emma St. Charles, the resident astronomer, lived half a mile down the hillside in a small house overlooking the ocean. She had two dogs for company and a plethora of birds who stuffed their bellies at her feeder. By night Emma watched the stars. By day she watched the birds. She was a delightful old scholar, a true observer of nature—human nature, too. Cat was very fond of her.

Cat got back into her car. In a minute or two Rob reappeared with a maroon blanket and a picnic basket. He leaned in and placed them carefully in the back seat. He'd put on a crisp blue shirt, which somehow made him look sexier than ever.

Climbing into the passenger's seat, he said, "Okay, lady, you got us: me, the food, and the wine. The ruthless Hepburn warrior is yours for the afternoon, to do what you will—or won't—with."

The faint air of confrontation seemed to have vanished completely. "Aha," she laughed, relaxing. "I think I hear my abused female ancestors clamoring for revenge. And you know how I'm going to take it?"

He solemnly shook his head.

"I'm going to see if I can't indoctrinate the skeptic into the Project Earth Society."

"Heaven help me," he groaned.

"For that matter, you never know . . . I might be an alien myself," she went on. "Are you sure you want to be alone with me? What if I've been waiting for a nice specimen of mankind to walk into my trap? I may carry you off to a distant galaxy and perform experiments upon you."

His eyes looked brown mischief into hers. "Experiments, huh?"

She sighed. That burning gaze of his was powerful enough to send a dozen UFO's hurtling into space. Face it, Catherine, she said to herself: If he's as vile a rogue and seducer as his ancestors were, you, my lass, are doomed.

Despite his laughing protests, they did discuss the Project Earth Society as they toured Aberdeen Island. Cat started by explaining that her grandfather had organized the group a couple of years ago after the death of her grandmother. "He needed something, you see. They had always been so close—one of the happiest couples I've ever known. When she died of cancer, Granddad went to pieces. I nearly did, too," she added sadly. "She'd been more of a mother than a grandmother to me."

Rob made a noise of sympathy; then Cat continued, "One night Granddad saw a mysterious sphere of light rising out over the woods in back of the castle, and it stimulated him to do some research into the subject of unidentified flying objects. Aberdeen Island has long been a focus of UFO activity. Granddad had had a couple of close encounters as a boy, and there are records of such events occurring regularly on the island for the past hundred years."

"Have you ever seen any?"

She shook her head. "I'm sorry to say I haven't. I feel a little left out, as a matter of fact." She stopped the car on the ocean road and pointed to a rocky outcrop of land being assaulted by the churning sea. "It was just off that point that Jon Hayden saw his UFO two nights ago. See the lobster pot markers bobbing out there? He was checking them when a large globe of light hovered nearby, then zipped off at high speed."

"Did anyone else see it?"

"No, just Jon."

"You know what we say about sightings witnessed by only one person, of course?"

"Hallucinations?"

"I'm afraid so. They might not be, of course, but for practical purposes, the only cases worth documenting are the ones with two or more reliable witnesses. And *reliable* is the operative word, believe me. Apart from the crazies seeing things that simply aren't there, there have been an appalling number of hoaxes perpetrated by clever liars who wanted a little publicity."

"Yes, I know, I've read about some of them. It must

be quite a task to separate the good data from the bad."

"It is," Rob confirmed. "The most difficult cases are the ones in which you have several honest, upstanding pillars of the community who all agree they've seen something bizarre. Sometimes they're quite embarrassed or even annoyed that they've seen it—they don't want to be thought crazy. But, good citizens that they are, they report it anyway."

"And?"

"And it usually turns out that the sighting is an easily explainable physical phenomenon. An airplane. A weather balloon. A satellite. A meteorite. An optical illusion."

"Don't forget the planet Venus," she said dryly. "I've read the Air Force's explanation of the Portage County Police Chase, in which several police officers independently sighted and chased a UFO that was as big as a house for eighty-five miles across Ohio and into Pennsylvania. The investigators later declared that the officers had been chasing Venus!"

Rob was glad he'd done his research on this subject. Cat MacFarlane was well-informed. "That explanation *was* a little farfetched."

"The trouble with most of you federal investigators is that you're biased from the start," Cat complained. "You assume that UFO's can't possibly exist, so you bend the facts until you come up with some sort of 'explanation.' Tell me, how scientific is that?"

"Not very," he was forced to concede.

As she drove him from place to place, describing the various UFO sightings, three quarters of Rob's attention—and sometimes all of it—was on the woman beside him. The rest was directed toward a survey of the island's geography—roads, hills, rocks, and fields. Quite simply, if there were smugglers on the island, they needed a place to land their planes. The only place he knew of was the old runway on Duncan MacFarlane's land. However, if there were other possible landing areas, he intended to be familiar with them.

From what he could see of the island, though, it was mostly pine forest and rocky hills. There was very little in the way of cleared, flat terrain. Bringing a plane in, even a small one, would not be an easy proposition.

He didn't raise the subject of the runway at first because he was curious to see whether Cat would take him there herself. She didn't. They had been touring for two hours, crisscrossing the small island on narrow dirt roads, when he casually asked her if she knew of any place to land a plane.

"Why?"

"I should have thought it would be obvious. What's the most likely cause of strange lights in the sky? Aircraft of some sort. Several of the sightings you've described— lights slowly rising out of the uninhabited middle area of the island accompanied by a soft throbbing noise— sound like small planes to me, Cat."

She looked distinctly uneasy. Guilty, perhaps? Rob felt something clench inside him. He wanted to believe in her innocence. He didn't want to do or say anything that would tend to confirm his less pleasant suspicions.

"There's no airport on the island," she said.

"But there *is* an airstrip," he said, his voice deceptively gentle. "Isn't there?"

For a second their eyes met in strained silence; then Cat answered, "I don't know if I would call it an airstrip, exactly, but there is a paved runway inland on my grandfather's property that has been used, occasionally, for landing planes. It was built during World War Two for military aircraft, but the war ended before the strip was finished. It hasn't been maintained, and very few people know it's there." She stopped and raised her eyebrows interrogatively. "How did you?"

"I have a U.S. Geological Survey map of the island,

drawn right after the war. The airstrip is noted on it."

"I see. Well, I'll take you there if you insist. But there's nothing much to look at."

"It's never used?"

"I've hired a pilot to fly me in now and then, for emergencies," she admitted. "During my grandmother's final illness, for instance." But she was thinking of another occasion entirely. Damn. She didn't want to go to the airstrip. It had been there that she'd seen Josh for the last time. They had indulged in a tender little parting scene—allegedly temporary, of course; then he had climbed back into his Piper Cub and left her still trusting him, still believing he was everything he'd claimed to be. It was not until a week later, when his cover had been blown, that he'd phoned and told her the truth.

"I would like to see it," said Rob.

And so they went. The runway was located in a short, flat valley between two wooded hills about half a mile away from her grandfather's castle and a similar distance from the sea. Since it was inaccessible except by foot, they hiked together over the hills, leaving the car parked on the blacktop near the ocean. The sun was hot, the air heavy and humid, and Cat was feeling rather impatient as she stood watching Rob pace off the length of the paved surface. He then bent down to examine the pavement for God-only-knew what.

"It hasn't been used for at least a year," she told him.

He didn't comment, although she thought his face seemed harder and more predatory than ever when he finally returned to her side.

The walk back to the coast road was hot and uncomfortable. Rob was brooding, and Cat was too full of unpleasant memories of the perfidy of Josh Evans to try to coax him into conversation. But when they came over the last rise into sight of the sea, her spirits rose once again. The wild power of the ocean always washed her clean of unhappy thoughts and emotions.

"I'm hungry," she said when they finally reached the car. "How about you, Rob?"

"Starved."

"I know a lovely spot near here for a picnic. Down there." She pointed to a narrow path that led toward the sea. "It's called Pirates' Cove, and it used to be my secret place." She smiled a little, adding, "Actually, it's still my secret place, a sort of fairyland—you'll see. But, of course, a scientist like you couldn't possibly believe in fairies."

"I suppose the fairies actually come from some other planet?" The teasing note was back in his voice.

"Grandfather thinks so. I'm not so sure."

Her fairyland was a beautiful place, Rob had to admit. It was a small meadow, bright with yellow, blue, and crimson wild flowers, sandwiched between two jutting sections of granite cliff. The grass came almost to the edge of a narrow cove of seawater, so they could spread out the blanket and sit only a few feet away from the pounding surf, feeling cut off and protected from the rest of the world.

Cat looked like a fairy creature herself as she settled down on the blanket, the sun making fiery ribbons of her breeze-tossed hair. While she was digging into the picnic basket for the food, Rob allowed himself the luxury of studying the figure she cut in her shorts—slender hips, long sun-tanned legs, and a tempting well-rounded bottom. Very nice. She was wearing running shoes over a pair of bright yellow socks that matched her blouse. The shoes would have looked unfeminine on most women, but for some reason they were adorable on her.

He closed his eyes briefly against the stab of desire that heated his vitals. What was it about this woman? Without doing anything particularly provocative, she'd raised his testosterone to record-high levels. He felt like a kid again, eager and undisciplined.

The worst of it was, he liked her. He didn't know

whether or not he could trust her—that airstrip had been used recently; he'd have staked his life on that—but the telltale signs of guilt or fear had not been evident in her demeanor when he'd insisted they investigate. *Something* about the place bothered her, though, he sensed. The reminder, perhaps, of her grandmother's illness and death? Now that they were away from there, she seemed her normal self again. She was sunshine personified: natural, easygoing, and quick with a smile. She was everything, in fact, that was missing in his life.

The thought electrified him for an instant. Then, deliberately and with a skill refined by long practice, he repressed his brief fantasy of romantic bliss.

"Tell me about yourself," he suggested as she dished out the French bread, cheese, tomatoes, and wine he'd provided. "You said you used to sing professionally. When and with whom?"

"You're going to be appalled," she predicted, taking an enormous bite of bread and cheese.

"Never."

"Okay—I was a rock star. Well, not quite a rock star. The group I sang with is very popular in Europe, but they've never quite made it in the U.S. Ever heard of the group Crusader?"

"I'm not into rock music," he hedged. He felt like a sleaze for asking her these questions. But he told himself he had to do it. Part of the job. Besides, he needed to hear her side. "You're not with the group anymore, I take it? Why'd you quit?"

For an instant he thought she wasn't going to answer. She frowned, sighed once, then slowly said, "There was an arrest—David Kineer, the lead guitarist. They got him for possession of marijuana. Somebody clearly wanted to make an example of him, so the case went to court. The ironic thing is that David wasn't guilty. He didn't use any kind of drugs. None of us did."

"I thought doing drugs was the normal way of life for

most people in the rock music business."

"Everybody thinks that, but it's not necessarily true. Drugs horrify me," she said with a shudder. "None of my friends ever used them."

"Except your friend David."

"That's just it." Her voice had darkened with anger. "He was set up, framed. There was an undercover spy hanging around the group, masquerading as a roadie, and—"

"What's a roadie?"

"One of the guys who moves the equipment and makes sure all the sound gear and instruments get safely to the next concert hall on the tour. Anyway, it turned out the guy was working for some federal agency. He was a bastard."

Cat's usually cheerful expression was so full of hate and anger that Rob felt a little sick. She was referring to Joshua Evans, his predecessor in the racket entitled Let's-deceive-Catherine-MacFarlane-about-our-real-jobs.

"I liked him," Cat went on tightly. She was twisting her gold necklace with a vengeance. "I had no idea he was a fed, no inkling he was out to further his career by busting David." She raised her head, and Rob saw the fires smoldering in her green eyes. "Josh—Mr. Evans—didn't get along with David, so he conceived a devious little plan to entrap him. Then, to make matters worse, he convinced *me* that David was doing drugs. He knew how strongly I felt about that. I got so angry with David that I quit the group and came home to the island. Oh, it wasn't just that—I was tired of the whole rock scene. But David thought I was abandoning him, and he's never forgiven me."

Rob didn't comment. He didn't like the way her voice broke when she mentioned David.

"I'd known him for a long time, you see," she went on, tugging at the necklace. "David's funny—not the easiest sort of person to be with, but . . ." She shrugged.

"All of us in the group were very loyal to one another. David couldn't understand why I left."

Probably worried she was on to him, thought Rob.

"I didn't find out until later that Evans was lying and that David had been innocent, after all. That swine set him up."

Rob's instinct was to argue, but he suppressed it. Cat seemed to have no suspicion of the real situation—that her precious friend David was into something a lot heavier than recreational drugs. Her blind spot about Kineer irritated him, but far stronger was his relief that she seemed to be so much in the dark about Evans's true role. It tended to confirm that agent's belief that Catherine was innocent of any involvement with the gunrunners.

"What happened to David?" he asked, although he knew.

"The judge gave him a suspended sentence, thank God. Poor David wouldn't have been able to bear being in prison; he's far too sensitive."

"Poor David," Rob echoed in a tone that bordered on the snide. Was she still in love with the jerk?

Cat shot Rob a quick look, noted his hard-mouthed expression, and decided it was time to change the subject. It wasn't something she wanted to pain herself by remembering, anyway—she'd wasted enough energy today brooding about that particular debacle.

It was funny, she thought suddenly, noticing how harsh Rob's expression had become. There was something about that tight-lipped sensuality, that watchful readiness, those lazy, hooded eyelids that reminded her of Josh.

She shivered slightly. Raising her cup, she took a large swallow of the dry red wine he'd brought along. This man, too, was a federal employee, she reminded herself. He might not be anything as devious as an undercover agent, but he was out to prove something, just as Josh had been. And like Josh Evans, he probably didn't give a damn whom he hurt in the process.

"What about you, Rob?" she inquired. "I don't know anything about your life. How long have you been chasing UFO reports? You said you were an astronomer. Do you spend any time in an observatory?"

"At a computer module, more frequently, analyzing data," he said smoothly, and proceeded, rather guiltily, to feed her more of his well-worked-out cover story. Some of it was true, of course; in particular, the details about his early career studying astrophysics at MIT. As for the rest, while they nibbled on their bread and cheese and sipped the wine, he attempted to bore her so thoroughly with talk of comets and pulsars and black holes that she would neglect to ask him about his more recent life. But, to his surprise and secret pleasure, she didn't seem the least bit bored.

"You know, I envy you," she said dreamily, stretching out on the blanket and running her fingers through the grass at one edge. "Sitting there in the dark of an observatory dome, staring for hours into the velvet depths of night."

He grinned. "You make it sound a lot more pleasant than it is. It's cold, for one thing, except in the middle of summer. And you get a stiff neck."

Unfazed, she continued, "When I was a little girl, Granddad used to take me up to the Aberdeen Observatory, and if she wasn't too busy, Emma would let us look through the telescope. It was wonderful! I remember looking at Jupiter and being astonished by its brightness. A shining round coin in the sky, surrounded with a dozen tiny moons. I felt as if I could reach out and cup my fingers around them."

Rob swallowed convulsively. He inched a little closer on the blanket, wanting very much to reach out and cup his fingers around *her*—that burnished hair, those soft, full lips, those small but enticing breasts. The sultry air, the wild summer setting, and the wine were all having their effect on him. And the woman, most of all the woman. *His* woman, he thought irrationally. He was going to make her his.

"Cat." The wind had come up suddenly; it tore away his whispered word. The sky had gone cloudy, the air heavy the way it grows before a storm. "Catherine," he said a little more loudly. She raised her head to meet his eyes. In one lithe movement he rolled over from his back to his stomach, propping himself up on one elbow. He was close to her now; he could smell her perfume, light and exotic as wild flowers. "Ye hae a way with words, lassie," he said, faking a Scottish accent. "Ye're a poet as well as a singer, are ye not?"

"Mmm," she said. A mysterious sparkle glimmered in her green eyes. "Would you like me to make up a poem about you?"

"By all means."

"Okay." She shut her eyes for a moment, and it was all he could do to restrain himself from kissing her soft, thick auburn lashes. But she opened them again before he could. "I've got it. Listen:

> "There once was a young man named Rob,
>   Chasing creatures from space was his job,
>   'It's a hoax,' he asserted—
>   'Twas the last word he blurted—
>   As he got swallowed up by the Blob."

Rob burst out laughing, and Cat grinned with pleasure. There it was, the laugh she'd been wanting to hear ever since she'd laid eyes on him. It was everything she'd hoped it would be—warm, husky, and full of vitality.

He looked like a different man when he laughed. The lines around his eyes fanned out, and there were actually two tiny dimples in his cheeks. Unselfconsciously, she reached out a finger to touch one of them, and the quality of his laughter changed. His eyes dilated, darkened, the brown of his pupils turned to smoky black.

"That's a limerick," he stated. "And limericks, I understand, are supposed to be bawdy."

"Oh, well, if it's bawdy you want, let me see, now . . ."

"There once was a lecherous Scot," he began helpfully.

Giggling, she plunged right in: "Whose desires waxed constantly hot."

"He fell for a redhead/And he, uh . . ." He faltered and stopped. "I'm not very good at poetry," he groused.

Inspired, she thought for a moment, then said, "Wait—I've got it:

> "There once was a lecherous Scot,
> Whose desires waxed constantly hot;
> He fell for a redhead,
> Whom he fain would have bedded,
> But the lady she wanted him not!"

"Bravo!" he laughed. In one smooth move he closed the distance between them, one arm coming down by the side of her head, one leg sliding over to press upon hers. "You're a liar, though, aren't you?"

She hardly breathed as his head came down. His nose rubbed hers; his fingers threaded through the silk of her hair. "I'm going to kiss you," he murmured. "No cavemen stuff, just a kiss. May I, sun-child?"

"Down, boy," she said softly, but she didn't mean it, and she knew he knew it. Smiling, she reached a hand up to cup the back of his neck and guided his mouth to hers.

CHAPTER FOUR

As Rob's mouth burned into hers, Cat's will to resist his seduction gave way to a stronger need. His mouth was hot, soft, and tender as it moved over hers. He didn't rush the kiss, nor did he take it too slowly. Without being overly aggressive, he made her subtly aware that he was in command.

He drew back for an instant to trace the shape of her mouth with his tongue. He stroked one corner, returned, stroked the other corner, then closed his teeth gently over her bottom lip. She moaned and shifted her legs restlessly. One of his hands came up to thread through her hair while his thumb rubbed erotically over her cheekbone. Her pulse was scampering, her breasts and belly aching. She tangled her fingers in his hair and pulled his face closer as he parted her lips and drove into her with his tongue.

They were gulping breath when he finally broke the kiss and raised his head to look into her eyes. "Siren," he murmured. He dropped several additional kisses on her eyelids and brow. "Green-eyed sorceress. I want to make love to you until we both see stars."

Oh, please do, she thought, but she managed to refrain from saying it out loud. She'd never felt such a strong attraction to any man before. Even so . . . Resolutely she pressed her palms against his strong shoulders. "It would be very nice, but I'm afraid I can't."

"Won't," he corrected, smiling.

"All right. Won't. Just a kiss—you promised."

"Because you're off men."

"Right," she said weakly, tempted, as she absorbed the heat of his body, to consign that particular resolution to hell.

His thumb continued to caress her, sliding from her cheek to the corner of her mouth. He swept it once over the damp surface of her bottom lip, and her body jumped with pleasure. Her eyes closed, and she felt his lips touch her lashes, heard his voice murmuring enticements. His body shifted beside her, his thigh pressing harder between her legs, his bent knee touching the zipper of her denim cutoffs. Such sweet torture! She could hardly prevent herself from arching against him.

"Do you mind telling me why you're off men?" he asked. "And how long you're intending to practice celibacy?" One hand moved over her throat and passed elusively down the front of her shirt, just missing her breasts. It lingered at her waist, then swept up her side until he touched a sensitive point under her arm. Good heavens, he was discovering erogenous zones she hadn't even known existed! "Will nothing induce you to change your mind?"

"Sorry, astronomer," she managed, smiling up at him. His brown eyes were dilated with passion, yet she thought she saw glimmers of good humor in them. "You'll just have to accept my no, without explanation."

"Remember I'm a Hepburn." He leered melodramatically. "Can't be trusted not to ravage and rape."

"If I'd believed that, I wouldn't have come out with you."

Something flashed in his face, harshly, then was gone. "Seems to me you don't know too much about me, sunchild. You'd better watch that. Somebody might take advantage of you someday."

Cat's eyes closed. "Somebody already has."

Reluctantly Rob levered himself up and eased slightly to the side. He had enough control to stop this now, but if he persisted, if he experienced for just a few more seconds the supple give of her flesh beneath his body, he'd lose it for sure. She felt so good. Her mouth. Her hair. Her thighs. She smelled like wild flowers and tasted like wine. She was brim-full of warmth and passion, but, like a walled garden, her treasures were ringed and well-guarded. The gates wouldn't open to just anybody who happened along.

Who had hurt her? he wondered. David Kineer? Rob's animosity for the man increased. He had yet to meet his adversary, but he already hated him.

Somewhere in the distance thunder cracked. Or maybe not so far in the distance. Cat's green eyes came open; her expression was honest and clear-sighted but faintly apologetic. "I don't think we'd better see each other again after today."

"Why?" The word was almost a curse.

"It's obvious: We have nothing to share but sexual attraction. I've been hurt by that before."

"Everyone's been hurt by that, Catherine. But the days of retiring to lead a celibate life in the convent are long gone. You're a vital young woman. You can't just give up men, sex, love." He frowned and added, "And frankly, from what I've seen of you so far, I would have expected you to have too much spirit to try."

"Oh, brilliant. Appeal to my spirit, not my body," she taunted him lightly. "It won't work, Rob. At least, not with you."

His gaze narrowed dangerously. "Why not with me? How am I different from other men?"

She fed her eyes on his lean and lanky body, the rich dark hair that was just a little too long in the back, the strong muscles rippling under the tan skin of his forearms. *You're infinitely more dangerous*, she was thinking. *You're harder and sexier and much more beautiful. You, more than most, could break me.*

"How long are you here for?" she said aloud.

"A couple of weeks only, but—"

She pressed her palms into the ground and sat up. "I think that answers your question, doesn't it? With another man there might be a chance for a relationship. I'm not interested in a two-week summer affair."

What could he say to that? He had nothing to offer her but a few transitory pleasures; that was all he'd had to offer any woman for the last several years. Affection, trust, love—other men sought and found these emotions, but Rob firmly believed they were dead in him. They'd died with Beth and been buried with her.

The thunder crashed more loudly now. Clouds were rolling in off the ocean, and a shining whip of lightning uncoiled across the darkened sky. "It's going to rain," he noted.

"A squall. It'll blow fiercely for a few minutes, then pass. They're common at this time of year."

He turned and looked at the steep path that led back up to the car. A fat raindrop struck his bare forearm, then another. "We'd better run for it."

Catherine was already tossing the lunch things back into the picnic basket. He rose and gave her his hand, which she gripped firmly, her smaller hand fitting comfortably in his. The rain was falling harder now; the thunder gathering around them. "We'll never make it," he added as he seized the blanket and crushed it against his chest.

"We won't make the car," she agreed. "There's shelter nearby, though. Follow me."

She ran lightly along the beach, heading for the farthest outcropping of stone in the narrow cove. Her hair seemed to glow with a nimbus of fire as the sky darkened further and the lightning forked into the ground. Unerringly she led him in against the cliff, around a massive rock, through a few inches of cold seawater to a crevasse in the cliff wall. At first it looked like nothing more than a fault in the cliff, but he realized as Cat ducked inside that there was a cavern there, tunneling deep into the jagged coastline.

They reached it just in time, too. No sooner did they slip under the overhanging rock than the sky opened up and the storm unleashed its full pagan fury. They were wet but not drenched; a few more seconds would have soaked them through. Cat's damp hair looked slightly darker than usual; when the lightning flashed it took on a mahogany sheen. Her eyes, too, were different—bigger, greener, as she stared out from the mouth of the cave at the emptying skies. She was breathing fast from their run . . . and from something else, a kind of primitive excitement that had to do with the strange leaden color of the sky, the sharp, sizzling quality of the air, and the sheer power of the storm.

"Look," she said, her tone hushed as she pointed out to sea. The wind had whipped the water into foam. Lightning bolts were striking so frequently that the entire surface of the water glowed with phosphorescence. It was an awesome, frightening storm, potentially lethal.

"I love it when it's like this," she added softly. "Look, it's almost as if the sea gods were battling the sky gods. Thunderbolts slam down, and waves heave upwards—

a monumental conflict between the elements."

"You're turning into a poet again."

She smiled. "Celebrating the beauties of nature? It *is* beautiful, isn't it?"

"A rather savage beauty," he said dryly. "I'd hate to be out there in a small boat."

She turned quickly, one warm hand touching his arm. "You're not afraid of thunderstorms, are you?" she asked.

He shook his head, touched by the obvious concern he could read in her eyes. "No."

"My grandmother was," she explained. "Terrified. We get them often here in the summer, and she hated it." She turned back to watch the dazzling show the elements were putting on. "I tried to understand, but I never could. To me it's uplifting, thrilling, magnificent. And how pointless to be afraid of such power."

Rob understood. You could resist a human enemy, but there was nothing you could do against the amoral battering of a storm. You could only accept it and let it take you where it would. There were emotions like that, he realized. It had been a long time since he'd felt them, but they were there, inside him. And suddenly they were clawing for release.

He stared at the woman beside him, her shining hair, her taut, slender body, her slightly parted lips, her huge, excited eyes. The age-old forces of nature were operating as much inside their shelter as outside. And suddenly it didn't matter that she'd said no to him only a few minutes before. Suddenly she was a different woman, and he a different man.

In an almost crippling upthrust of desire Rob swayed toward her, catching her shoulders between his palms and pressing her back against the damp rock wall of the cave. Her green eyes registered surprise as he bent his head to take her mouth, but only for an instant. He saw the flare of her own desire; then her eyelids closed, and she was kissing him just as wildly as he was kissing her.

And he was lost. A man of discipline and control, he was blasted into near-violence by the warmth of her response. They melted into each other; then he was dragging her down, down to the cold, rough floor of the cave. With some vestige of ancient masculine chivalry he resisted the urge to press her sweet body beneath his own; instead he went first, half-reclining with his back against the wall and his legs stretched out on the rocky floor. She came down on top of him, her hair a fiery curtain around her shoulders, her light and delicate body protected from the harsh environment by his own. And once again he plundered her lips, not thinking, not questioning, only *feeling*.

Cat was just as swept away as he was. One minute she was standing watching the storm, and the next she was lying willingly across Rob Hepburn's lap on the floor of the cave, crying out under his fierce, demanding caresses. It was not a seduction, for there was no subtlety involved; it might almost have been an attack, except that she was no less eager than he. There was nothing in her experience to compare with this wild explosion of passion. It was mindless, inarticulate, chaotic. She wanted him, and she had somehow been transformed into an abandoned creature whose sensual desires came before any other consideration.

Thunder cracked and lightning flickered as Rob threaded kisses along her jawline, nipped the pulse in her throat, rubbed his nose along the gold thread of her necklace. He was cradling her in his arms, one upthrust knee supporting her back while his head nuzzled her throat and breasts. He was over her, under her, all around her, it seemed. And he was murmuring incoherent praise against her heated skin, words that had no meaning yet were understood. He was like the storm—swift, savage, unstoppable, irresistible.

Cat's spine arched as his hands forced her shirt up to

bare her breasts to his sight. "Beautiful," he crooned, his breath whispering against her dampening skin. Reverently he stroked one nipple with his index finger while he bent his head to its twin and suckled her gently. Cat moaned deep in her throat and shivered all over. Beneath her hip she could feel the fierce swell of his arousal. He was all man—strong, potent, and deliciously masterful. She loved his musky masculine scent, the rough texture of his skin, the black silk of his hair beneath her fingertips. She loved the way he was cradling her body, his efforts to be protective of her and tender even in the throes of violent passion.

"Sweetheart," he murmured, dabbing her breast with the tip of his tongue. He let her feel his teeth on the rosy brown areola, hard enough to make her gasp at the intense pleasure-pain. Then he drew her nipple into his mouth while his hand drifted down over her taut belly and inside the waistline of her denim shorts.

If she was going to stop him, she thought vaguely, it had better be now. But she didn't want to stop him. She didn't want to think, and so, for once, she didn't. His fingers had already found the snap of her jeans and dealt with it; she heard a whisper of sound as he eased her zipper down. Automatically, by instinct almost, she opened her lips to make a restraining sound, but her protest was silenced by another devastating kiss.

She felt the heat of his hand on her bare skin. Delving under her silky bikinis, he rubbed erotically, tangling his fingers in the curls between her legs. She turned boneless in his arms. It felt so good, so right. It was pure joy, pure heaven.

His tongue thrust in rhythm with his fingers, and Cat was dazzled by the beauty and passion of his touch. "Move with me . . . that's it . . . yes," he murmured, stroking her harder, faster. Panting, shivering, she allowed him to coax her deeper and deeper into hot silken pleasure. "Sweet, sweet, my golden girl, yes!"

The storm outside still raged, but now it was part of herself, part of him. And she was riding the lightning, shuddering with the thunder, and coming apart in his arms. She cried out ecstatically as she felt the sharp liquid pulses of release. Then she was clinging to him, kissing his chest and murmuring her delight while he continued to caress her and bring her safely down.

Endless moments later Cat opened her eyes. The squall had subsided; the time between each flash of lightning and each corresponding crack of thunder had grown longer. She lifted her cheek from Rob's shoulder and leaned back to see his face, which was dark, angular, and a little harsh in the darkness of the cave. A stranger's face. An erotic demon's face. She blushed. *Oh, dear heavens, what have I done?*

He leaned down to nuzzle her hair. "Okay?" he whispered.

"Uh, wonderful," she said shakily. "Thank you."

His grin was a white slash in the darkness. "My pleasure." He lifted her carefully—she was still sprawled across his lap—moving her a little to the side. "I've got the blanket bunched up here; let me spread it out. The floor's rather hard and cold, I'm afraid. It might be dryer deeper inside the cave, but we haven't got a flashlight, and I don't know how far back it goes."

"It's a huge cave, and quite safe, I understand," she said mechanically. *Spread out the blanket? For what? More lovemaking?* She glanced nervously at the front of his jeans, which were far too tight to hide the fact that his release was yet to come. Awkwardly she pulled her blouse down, covering her breasts once again, wondering what on earth to say. She was assailed by her own very strong sense of fair play. She'd had her turn; now it was his.

No, she reminded herself. *This needn't go any further. If you don't want the rest of it, he'll just have to accept that.*

The only trouble was, she wasn't sure whether she wanted it or not. He was handsome, gentle, and very sexy. He had beautiful, dark, expressive eyes, and his hands could work magic. She'd already learned that he was a skilled and considerate lover. Why not, for god-sake? Why the hell not?

Because you don't love him, an indignant voice prodded. You hardly even *know* the man!

He spread out the blanket and turned to her. Even in the darkness, Rob could read the disquiet in her eyes. *Damn.* She was withdrawing; he felt it—he was losing her. And that was a prospect he couldn't bear. His body was afire for her. He didn't think he could let her go.

He offered her his hands, trying to hide his own sudden dismay. Smart, buddy. You should have played it cagier—withholding her pleasure until you were certain of your own. "Second thoughts?" he asked quietly, tipping her head back with one finger under her chin.

She nodded. "I'm sorry," she murmured.

He took her hand and pressed it to himself, almost groaning under the heat of her touch. "That's what you do to me. That and a lot more that's not so palpable. I need you, sun-child. Don't shy away from me now."

She removed her hand slowly, wanting neither to insult him nor encourage him further. She had to block her feminine awareness of how very nice he felt. The thought of *that* against her . . . inside her . . . "I'm sorry," she repeated in a strangled tone. "It's unforgivable of me, I know. My only excuse is that I've never lost my head like that . . . I don't know how it happened."

"Don't you?" They were kneeling opposite each other, but as she absorbed the intensity of his gaze, she clumsily groped for the wall, anxious to resume her shaky legs again. Rob caught her wrist, preventing her, his fingers an unbreakable band. "I'll show you how it happened," he added, forcing her against him once more and bringing his mouth down to hers.

He didn't hurt her, but his tension shot through both
of them as Cat warily acknowledged the anger of the
thwarted male. His kiss was different this time—more
primitive, more possessive. It was the way he'd kissed
her last night in front of her grandfather—the sweeping
embrace of a Hepburn warlord. It was both a challenge
and a claim.

Instinct warned her not to fight him, lest her struggles
excite his masculine need to dominate. She had to force
herself not to respond, either, because his body felt hard
and lean and oh-so-temptingly-good against hers. When
at last he lifted his mouth and enigmatically met her eyes,
she swallowed hard and said, "Please don't, Rob. No
caveman stuff, you promised."

There was a pause while they both heard her words.
She felt him relax infinitesimally against her. "That was
before you led me into your cave, woman," he growled.

She smiled, then laughed aloud. He kissed her again,
a good deal more tenderly. "Cathy," he whispered against
her lips. Once again she began to melt. Many years ago
her father used to call her Cathy. Something about the
nickname made her feel protected and cherished. "Love
me," he added.

Love me. But it wasn't love this seductive devil wanted
from her; it was sex. A fleeting two-week affair. No,
that wasn't cherishing—that was *using*. "I'm not in the
habit of making love with strangers," she informed him.

"Am I such a stranger to you? We haven't known each
other long, it's true, but there's already a kind of instinctive trust between us, Catherine. I feel it. You must,
too."

She slid her fingers along his arms to his shoulders,
not meaning it as a caress but feeling his muscles tense
and shiver beneath her touch and seeing a flash of agony
in his eyes. Guiltily she dropped her hands into her lap.
Her zipper was still open, she discovered. Blushing again,
she did it up. "I've learned the hard way how delicate

an emotion trust is," she told him. "I used to just accept people, never fearing they were out to hurt, use, or deceive me. But my last lover did all three of those things to me and more. It never occurred to me not to trust him. But now, because of him, I'm a little dubious about trusting you."

Rob swore aloud. "Your last lover. David Kineer, you mean?"

Cat's green eyes narrowed slightly as she shook her head. "David and I were never lovers," she said. "My last lover was the man who arrested him." Her voice dropped as she added, "The undercover spy."

"*Evans* was your lover?"

"Yes, Josh Evans."

"Dammit to hell," Rob muttered under his breath.

CHAPTER FIVE

"I WAS VERY foolish," Cat explained dispassionately. "Josh turned out to be a man of facades, a man of lies. He was just doing his job, he informed me later—as if that made everything all right. He was cold and pragmatic about the promises he'd made me, the words of love he'd spoken. I'd been the vulnerable member of the group, you see. The person who was most likely to reveal the juicy details about the drug orgies my friends were supposedly involved in. So he seduced me."

Rob made a sound in his throat that Cat misinterpreted as skepticism. "Oh, I was willing—I don't deny that," she said. "I was neither overly young nor overly innocent, but I was no match for James Bond. I fell very hard, I'm afraid. He was"—she paused—"very experienced, very sensual, very persuasive." Her eyes met his with a touch of defiance. "In some ways he was a lot like you."

Rob jerked to his feet, controlling, with difficulty, an urge to slam his fist into the wall. He'd never met Evans, but he felt like killing him. Yet it was misdirected aggression, he knew. Evans had seduced and abandoned a warm, sweet-tempered young woman who didn't deserve that kind of treatment. And yet Rob had been on the verge of doing exactly the same thing himself.

"And you know what made it even worse?" she went on. "Josh admitted to me in the end that he'd suspected me all along. Even while we were sleeping together, he believed I might be some kind of criminal! 'I had to be sure you were innocent,' he told me, as if there had ever been any doubt! 'I can rest easy,' the bastard declared, 'now that I know you're in the clear.' Do you *believe* that?" She cursed softly. "To this day I don't understand how I could have been so blind to the man's true character!"

"He was a good actor," Rob said hoarsely.

"The best."

"Guys who work undercover have to be, Cat. That kind of work is tricky. If his cover had been blown, it could have meant his life."

"Malarkey! He wasn't in any danger, and all that happened when his cover *was* finally blown was that he had to quit the case."

Abruptly realizing his comments might reveal too much, Rob took a different tack. "You know, now that you mention it, I think I remember this story. Was Evans the one whose picture was splashed all over the papers last summer?"

"That's right. That was David's doing—his revenge, I guess you could say. The rock music press is very liberal, and they were delighted to publish David's photos of a genuine narc. The story was picked up by a lot of other papers, some of whom probably got into trouble for running Josh's picture. It apparently played havoc with his career."

"You don't sound too sympathetic."

"Why should I be? He hurt me badly and set David up!"

Rob said nothing. His head was aching slightly at the temples. Since no one had informed him, he wondered for the first time what Evans was doing now. Morton had suspected Evans of having a soft spot for Catherine MacFarlane; he might have cared more deeply about her than Cat realized. Nothing had come of it, of course. The Agency tended to discourage that sort of thing.

Cat was giving him a sour look. "I forgot," she said. "You work for the government, too, investigating people, destroying their illusions. I don't suppose I can expect you to see it from my perspective. You and Josh are fellow hunters, fellow predators."

Rob cursed out loud, feeling all the more guilty because she didn't realize how accurate she really was. Good God! This would have to end, right here, right now. As much as he wanted her, as much as it tore out his guts to deny himself the pleasure of her warmth, her laughter, he was going to have to give up the chase. Evans had backed off, and he must do the same. Better now than later, for his own sake as much as for hers. Better he wrap up his investigation as quickly as possible and get the hell out of her life.

The possibility of having her find out that he, too, was an undercover agent, that he, too, had lied to her, that he, too, had suspected her of a crime suddenly seemed too grim to contemplate. She'd been hurt enough. Besides, the fact that he was so concerned about hurting her disturbed him. The fact that he gave a damn. He didn't know her well enough to give a damn, so why this guilt? Why this ache at the thought of never seeing her again?

"Rob?" Cat's voice was soft, uncertain. She touched his arm gently. "I shouldn't have said that. I don't get angry easily, but when I do, I sometimes overreact. I'm sorry. You're not really like Josh."

It had been a long time since Rob had felt more like a bastard. With a ragged sigh, he reached down and covered her hand with his. "No, you're right, Cat. Don't apologize. I was going to take what I could get, then walk away. I'm the one who's sorry, lady."

"I guess I couldn't have blamed you," she said. She gave him a rueful smile. "I gave you an emphatic *no* outside, then came in here, and . . . I'm really sorry, Rob. It's just that sex has always been a serious matter for me. When you perform the way I did, singing sexy songs, living on the road for months at a time with a group of young and virile men, it's tempting to get casual, to forget the values you learned as a kid, to take the easy road of booze and pills and who-the-hell-cares sex. I had to fight not to get seduced by that lifestyle. I succeeded, but not without personal cost—friends who thought I was a kill-joy, men who concluded I must be a 'frigid bitch.'"

He touched her flaming hair gently. "You're certainly neither of those."

"Josh was a way to cut loose, to be passionate and wild and free. To soar like a bird—until he shot me down."

"Is that how it ended—he shot you down?"

"Yes. He called to say he was a special agent whose cover had just been blown. That he couldn't see me anymore. That he didn't really love me." She paused a moment, then added, "He didn't even have the gumption to tell me in person. He might have been a tough-guy spy, but he didn't have the guts to face me. He broke up with me by phone!"

There was probably a good reason for that, Rob knew. If Evans's photograph was about to be splashed in newspapers across the country, the Agency would have deep-sixed him for a while. Cat was lucky to have received so much as a phone call.

"I was devastated," she went on. "I wasn't wild and free at all, you see. I wanted love, the kind of love I'd been offering him. I can't just give my body. Once I start, I give everything, and I expect my partner to do the same." She tilted back her head to see his eyes. "Do you understand?"

"I hear you, Cathy, yes." One finger brushed a fiery strand of hair back from her face. "You're a warm and giving woman, and I wish to hell I had more to offer you than a ready body and some broken illusions. But I don't."

She tugged at her necklace and did not speak.

"So don't trust me any more than you trusted Evans. All I'm capable of giving any woman is sensual pleasure. I don't know how to love, and I don't think I'm capable of learning."

Wordlessly she went into his arms, feeling absurdly close to tears. For him, for herself. "That's sad, Rob," she murmured. "If it's true, I feel sorry for you." She hesitated a moment, then asked, "But how can you say such a thing—you don't know how to love? Haven't you ever loved anybody?"

Rob shrugged.

Cat wondered if she dared question him about his dead wife. Presumably he had loved *her*. Was he someone who, having lost everything once, was reluctant to risk losing again?

It struck her that he had not been very forthcoming. She knew next to nothing about his personal life. She'd talked, but he hadn't. Most of what he had told her during lunch about his past work as an astronomer had been highly technical. He'd told her nothing to give her any real flavor of his life—nothing about his childhood or his family, nothing of his hopes, his dreams, his aspirations.

Yet, on some deep level, she felt as if she knew him. Was it because of the silent communication that arced between them when his expressive eyes locked with hers? Was it something in the warm and husky timbre of his voice, or in the indecipherable language of his body? Was it because of the protective, considerate way he made love?

"I was burned by Josh," she tried, wondering if a reminder of how much he knew about *her* would help to loosen his tongue. "But it wouldn't stop me from trying again if the right man came along."

"I'm not the right man, Cat," was all he said. "I wish I were."

She sighed. If Rob Hepburn didn't want to let his barriers down, that was his decision. And perhaps he was right not to. If their relationship had no future, what point would there be in striving for better communication, better understanding?

She couldn't think of anything else to say. For several moments they sat without moving, without touching, side by side against the wall of the cave. Then Rob turned to embrace her once again, his fingers running feverishly through her hair, as if it were the last time. Which it probably was, she realized miserably.

"Come on, sun-child. Let's get out of here before we get into any more trouble, okay?"

She nodded and let him pull her to her feet.

Outside it was still raining, but the worst of the storm had passed. The thunder was far in the distance now, and the lead-gray of the sky was fading as the clouds moved off to the east.

Rob walked right out into the rain. Cat took the blanket from him and followed, draping it over her head. She was feeling a little dazed still; grateful, yes, that he'd listened to her and accepted her story about Josh as an excuse to avoid further intimacy, while at the same time the tiniest bit miffed—perversely, she knew—that he'd been so easy to dissuade. He was a far more honorable man than Josh, she was certain. Either that, or he simply didn't want her as much.

For Josh had wanted her—that she had never doubted.

He'd used her, yes, and lied, and ultimately he'd walked away, but there had never been anything artificial about his passion. It was only his love that had been a sham.

Passion, at least, was *something*.

"You can share my umbrella, if you like," she offered, waving a flap of the blanket in Rob's direction.

He stopped and held his arms out to the fresh summer rain. "No, thanks. I need this. It's the closest thing to a cold shower I can find at the moment."

She smiled as she noted that his jeans still had a long way to go to regain a shape that was fit for polite company. Rob's passion, too, was real, she acknowledged. For the first time in her life she wished she were the type of woman for whom passion was enough. "There's the ocean. You could go for an icy swim."

"I want to cool off, not permanently incapacitate myself," he retorted. "And if you don't stop looking so smug, MacFarlane, you'll be the one taking a dive."

Her smile dissolved into a laugh. Yes, he reminded her of Josh, with his sensuality and tough masculinity, but the truth was, he was a pleasanter man than Josh had ever been. Josh had never laughed with her, teased her, or joked around. Josh had not been such an exciting— and yet unselfish—lover, either, she recalled, feeling the blood heat her face again. Damn Josh, anyway!

The ride back to the observatory was subdued and uncomfortable. Rob wished he'd been driving; it would have given him something else to concentrate on besides his awareness of her hands on the wheel, her legs tensing as she depressed the accelerator and the clutch, her breasts, her thighs . . . Damn! In desperation, he asked her several more questions about the UFO sightings, trying his best to focus on the information she obligingly provided. But his thoughts kept flashing back to the sweet, abandoned way she'd responded to the coaxing of his hand between her legs.

When she stopped the car in front of the white-domed building at the top of the hill, Rob took his blanket and picnic basket and climbed out of the car. "Your grand-father can relax," he said tightly. "This Hepburn isn't going to try to seduce you again."

She held his gaze for only a moment, then looked away, her green eyes shimmering with moisture. Jeez— tears? He wanted to fold her close and comfort her; he wanted to caress her gently all over and bring that bright, delightful smile back to her face. Right, Hepburn, the darker side of him mocked. What you really want is her naked body straining beneath you in bed.

"Good-bye, Rob," she said.

"Good-bye, sun-child."

He watched her car drive off down the hill, following it with his eyes until it disappeared behind the curve of the rocky shore road. He stood there, staring out to sea like an idiot, wondering about love and relationships and all he was missing, until he caught himself up with a sneer. "You've got work to do, buddy; this isn't a va-cation," he said out loud. "You've gotta go over this godforsaken rockpile of an island with the proverbial fine-toothed comb."

One thing, at least, was settled to his satisfaction: Cat MacFarlane was not a gun-smuggler. He'd bet his life on that.

CHAPTER SIX

FIVE DAYS PASSED without a word from Rob. Not that Cat had expected to hear from him. In fact, she'd convinced herself that it would be disastrous to hear from him, even though she thought of him, fantasized about him, dreamed of him, constantly. Her songs were full of him . . . when she could write at all. She started several new compositions but found it impossible to finish any of them. Her music, her poetry, was half-written, unconsummated, like her potential love affair with Rob.

Which left her with a problem on her hands. She'd promised Adrian Andrews, who'd produced all Crusader's recent recordings, that she'd have the material for her second LP finished before the summer was over so they could start recording in September. She'd already done one solo LP, which would be coming out shortly, and Adrian was predicting great success for her. Her voice, he claimed, had a highly unusual quality, and the lyrics and harmonies of her songs a wide appeal.

Cat was too sophisticated in the vagaries of the music business to take all this too seriously. On the other hand, she could use the advance the next record would bring her. She hadn't earned very much in the past year.

One morning she was in Aberdeen, the small fishing village that was the closest thing to a metropolis the island had to offer, dropping her latest not-so-hot material in the mail for Adrian. She was leaning against her car, waiting for her grandfather to finish an errand in the bank, when she saw Rob Hepburn come out of the local grocery store. He crossed the street in front of her, not seeing her, and she thought he was going to disappear into his own car without a word when he suddenly stopped and turned, as if he'd been moved by the simple power of her eyes upon him.

The shock of their gazes locking shook Cat from head to toe. He was dressed casually again, in painted-on jeans and a blue work shirt. His skin was more tan than it had appeared last week, and his smile was a flash of white as he acknowledged her and started toward her car. Heavens, he was quite a man—a lean, lanky, smooth-moving, sexy-eyed hunk of masculinity. And you turned him down? You're a real dummy, Cat MacFarlane!

"Hi." He came over and rested one hip against her car.

"Hi, Rob. You're still here, huh?"

"Yup. Still here." His eyes paid tribute to her legs.

"Uh, how's it going?" Smart, Catherine. What conversation, what wit. How's it going, indeed!

"Okay. How's it going with you?"

She smiled as she realized he felt as awkward as she. "Nice weather we're having, isn't it?" she said impishly.

"There's a storm predicted for tomorrow," he observed.

"We get a lot of storms at this time of year."

"Yeah, I know—something to do with warm fronts

and cold— What the hell are you laughing about?"

"I was just wondering how long we could talk about the weather."

A grin loosened up his features. "I could think of other things I'd rather do with you than talk, Cat MacFarlane. You wanna change your mind?"

"Uh, no, I don't think so."

"Anytime you do, I'll be ready," he said huskily, making it clear, from a quick glance down at the front of his jeans, that she knew exactly what he meant by *ready*.

"Rob, for godsake!"

His eyes danced, but he changed the subject with barely a pause in the flow of words between them. "I've been talking to your various witnesses about the UFO's. The only one who's got anything particularly interesting is that lobsterman, Jon Hayden. If he really saw what he thinks he saw—a shining globe of light that actually played some sort of music before zipping off at great speed—we just might have something. Too bad he was the only witness."

"He's reliable, though, Rob," she said, excited. "He doesn't drink or anything, and he's—" She broke off as she noticed that Rob's attention had shifted to a point just behind her. She turned her head. Her grandfather had come out of the bank and was advancing on the car.

"Cat!" he growled, as if she were a child engaged in some sort of mischief.

Cat straightened. "Are you finished, Granddad? You remember Mr. Hepburn," she said stiffly.

"Aye, I remember him all right. I told you not to have anything further to do with the man!"

"Don't blame her, MacFarlane," Rob said. "She's very distant with me, I assure you. I was the one who accosted her. In true Hepburn style."

Duncan MacFarlane came around the back of the car to face Rob, looking only slightly less belligerent than he'd been the night they met. "Well, if you don't want trouble with me, young man, you'll pay more heed to my command to keep away from her," he snorted. He had taken up a spread-legged stance, and his arms were hanging loosely at his sides, hands balled into fists. The masculine challenge was as old as time. And its ludicrousness was even more apparent in the light of day than it had been that night at the castle: Rob was taller, stronger, and in the prime of his manhood. There was no real contest between them. All her grandfather had going for him was his pride.

Don't break that pride of his, Cat pleaded silently with Rob. *Don't taunt him the way you did that first night, when you kissed me in front of him.*

Rob's eyes flickered to her briefly, giving her no indication whether or not he sensed her plea. His face was impassive as he said to her grandfather, "I don't want trouble with you, sir."

Oh, you darling. Granddad looked slightly taken aback. "Then clear off, Hepburn," he said.

"What I would like is for this infernal clan feud to come to an end. Whatever my ancestors did, it's in the past. Surely you and I, as civilized modern men, can contrive to make peace between ourselves?"

"So you can use your villainous wiles on my granddaughter?" MacFarlane half shouted. "What kind of fool do you take me for?"

Rob shot Cat a look that said, *I tried.*

"I've heard what you're here for, Hepburn," Granddad stormed on. "I've heard the way you've been asking questions all over the island about Project Earth. Mocking and making sport of us, with the intent of writing up your *scientific* findings in some effete journal or government report. Well, you know what I think of your type, Hepburn? You know what I think of skeptical, know-it-all investigators like you?"

"I can guess," Rob said dryly.

"Granddad, let's go," Cat urged, taking his arm and trying to get him into the car.

"You're a challenge, that's what you are," MacFarlane said, somewhat to Cat's surprise. She'd expected something nastier. "You're one of the things that makes Project Earth so stimulating. How do we convert the disbelievers, the ones who come to mock? That's the real problem facing our group."

Rob's eyebrows went up. "You know, MacFarlane, I'm beginning to think you're enjoying this. The lecherous Hepburn is threatening your granddaughter, while at the same time the rational scientist is threatening your precious UFO's. I'll bet your life hasn't been this exciting in months."

"Rob!" Cat protested.

But instead of taking further umbrage, her grandfather simply raised his chin at Rob and smiled defiantly. "I'll go the distance with you, Hepburn, that I promise you."

Rob nodded as if he were taking him perfectly seriously. "May the best man win," he said.

Cat puzzled over these new developments as she drove her grandfather back to the castle. There was something zestful about the conflict between the two men, she realized. And Rob was right: Her grandfather hadn't been so frisky in months. And as for her . . . She remembered how sexy Rob had looked in those too-tight jeans, and she unconsciously indulged in the deep-chested sigh for which frustrated lovers are justly famous.

"You're not brooding over that Hepburn devil, I hope?" Duncan MacFarlane demanded. "Have you been seeing him? After I specifically ordered you not to?"

"Really, Granddad, aren't I a little old to be ordered about?"

"What are you up to, lass? You look as guilty as you

used to look as a teenager when I caught you getting up to some mischief or other."

She shot him a sidelong grin. "I'm not up to anything, I promise you." Rather the contrary, she was thinking. If she were up to something, she'd undoubtedly be feeling a lot less irritable.

"I saw the way you were staring at him. Making sheep's eyes, like a fool in love," he informed her. "And as for the way he was looking at you . . . The fact is, I'm getting pretty damn suspicious!"

"Look, Granddad, I really don't want to discuss this anymore. Suspicious or not, you're simply going to have to respect my privacy where members of the opposite sex are concerned."

"I've tried respecting your privacy. I didn't say anything when you fell head over heels for that snake Josh Evans, did I? Even though I knew the man was no good, I kept my opinions to myself. And I regretted it afterward, honey, believe me. If I'd spoken my mind, maybe you'd have listened and not been so badly hurt."

"I doubt it," Cat said wryly. "That was one lesson I had to learn on my own."

"You're too trusting by far, Cat. You're so busy looking for the good in people that you pass over all the evil." He squeezed her hands in his. "I'm getting old, lassie. Soon I'll be dead. I want to see you happy first, though. I don't think I can bear to see you hurt again."

"You're not old!" she insisted fiercely. "And don't you dare talk about dying."

"Since your grandmother went, lass, I don't have much reason to stick around. You're the only thing keeping me here, Catherine. If I knew you had a good man to take care of you, I'd feel easier about leaving to join my Meg."

Cat didn't view a man to protect her as the ultimate in human happiness, but she knew better than to argue the point. Her grandfather was old-fashioned in that re-

spect. Anyway, perhaps he was right. If she had a man—
a lover or a husband—she wouldn't be susceptible to
the wiles of a passing stranger like Rob Hepburn. She
was a normal woman with normal desires for sex, for
love, for companionship. Being "off men" wasn't going
to get her any of those things.

She tossed her head and said lightly, "I'll never find
that man if you forbid me to socialize, Granddad. It's
bad enough that I live in a fortress, without the laird of
the castle calling down curses and threatening to murder
my suitors!"

"Catherine, you can't have a Hepburn as a suitor! The
very prospect sends chills through my blood. The men
of that clan are devils incarnate, lassie. They're liars and
betrayers; you mustn't trust 'em!"

"He's not a suitor," Cat said with another sigh. "He's
wrapping up his investigation, and in a few days he'll
be gone. So you see, there's really nothing for you to
worry about."

Her grandfather scowled but said no more.

Somehow she knew when the telephone rang late that
night that it would be Rob on the other end. She hesitated
before she picked it up. "Hello?"

"Hi," he said.

"Rob." She couldn't deny the thrill that ran through
her entire body. She smiled. "Nice weather we're having,
huh?"

"Look, lady, every day I've forced myself not to call
you, but after seeing you in town today . . . I don't know
. . . I no longer had the willpower to keep my fingers off
the phone."

"Oh, Rob," she said softly.

"I want to be with you, Cat. It's really killing me to
be on the same island with you and never see you. Tomorrow's Saturday. Come out somewhere with me."

"No. I can't."

"Won't," he corrected.

"You know what'll happen if I do."

He laughed harshly. "I know what I keep fantasizing about every minute of the day. I can't stop remembering how it felt to hold you, kiss you, run my fingers through your flaming hair, touch your breasts . . . kiss them . . . hear your pleasure sounds—"

"I'll hang up," she threatened.

"You won't." She could hear the smile in his voice. "You're too turned on."

"Oh, really, Mr. Know-it-all?"

"Yeah. Aren't you?"

Oh, what the hell? "Yes," she admitted. "You definitely turn me on, Hepburn."

He groaned. "Cat, this is crazy. I want you, dammit! It's not even normal wanting—it's some kind of obsession. Ever since I heard you sing. You're a real-life Siren. You've put a spell on me." His own voice dropped seductively. "Tomorrow. We'll go for another picnic, or, if you prefer, we could rent a sailboat for the weekend. Sail over to the mainland. We'll find a nice restaurant, a night spot, a quiet hotel. Or we could get on a plane and fly down to Boston or Manhattan for a night on the town. Whatever you want, Cat. Whatever would give you pleasure."

"Very tempting," she said in a voice that wasn't as lighthearted as she meant it to be. "Why do I have the feeling my MacFarlane ancestors heard similar promises from their Hepburn admirers?"

"Damn you, Catherine! You and your blasted grandfather. I'm serious."

"I know," she whispered. "But the answer's still no."

"Why, dammitall?"

"Because you're not serious *enough*. Nothing has changed, Rob. Nothing *can* change. I've been miserable without you, too, but it doesn't compare to the way I'd feel if I loved you, then lost you a week from now."

He swore viciously.

"Watch your mouth, Hepburn," she said, smiling. "Good night."

"Don't you dare hang up—" he began, but it was too late; she already had.

Two miles away in the Aberdeen Observatory Rob Hepburn slammed down the phone and all but ripped it off the wall. "Bitch! I'm damned if I'll ever call you again."

About thirty seconds later he was dialing. "Listen," he said when she picked up her end. "You know what the Hepburns do when the MacFarlane women resist their most seductive blandishments?"

"What?"

"We attack. Scale the walls. Bust down the doors. Break into milady's bedchamber, that sort of thing."

She laughed. "Don't get carried away, please. If you tried to scale these walls, you'd probably break your neck—if my grandfather didn't clout you with his broadsword first."

"I'll have you know that I'm an expert wall-scaler. Particularly when the incentive's so great."

"You're a madman, you know that?"

"Mmm. An excess of sex hormones has changed the chemistry in my brain. You're my only cure, Catherine."

"This is great," she laughed. "I haven't heard lines like these since high school."

"Yeah, well, when the men in the white coats come to take me away, I'm gonna be screaming your name."

Inspiration seized her, and she couldn't resist. "There once was a lecherous Scot," she began.

"Uh-oh."

"Shh. Just listen:

> "There once was a lecherous Scot
> Whose hormones burned sensually hot,
> To his lady he pleaded,

'Please take me, I need it,
Or my wits'll diminish to naught.'"

He laughed delightedly. "And what did the cruel lady say to that?"

"Hmm, let me see . . . 'There once was an innocent maid'—"

"No way," he interrupted. "Try again, *woman*."

"'There once was a hardhearted dame'?"

"That's more like it. Go on."

"'There once was a hardhearted dame,/ Whom no man could saddle or tame'—"

"*Saddle?* We're getting bawdy here, aren't we?"

"You ain't seen nothin' yet."

"No? Try me."

"There once was a hardhearted dame,
Whom no man could saddle or tame,
She said when they tried,
'You're not coming inside,
That's the number one rule of the game.'"

Rob was howling now. "You should be ashamed of yourself. An innocent maid, indeed. I blush for you."

"Rob?"

"Yeah, sun-child?"

"I appreciate your patience with my grandfather this morning."

"That's okay. I felt a sudden ungovernable liking for the balmy old Scot."

"You were right, I think: He's enjoying this conflict with you."

"Yeah? Maybe I should escalate it, then. Carry his granddaughter off and debauch her."

"You, sir, are very good at threats."

"Cat—"

"What did you mean the other day when you said you didn't know how to love?"

Rob was jolted by the sudden change of mood and subject. Over his head, the vast dome of the observatory opened its doors to the deep night sky as Emma began her work for the night. For an instant he seemed to feel the coldness of space permeating his very flesh and bones. "I don't know," he said.

"May I ask you something? When did your wife die?"

"Eight years ago."

"How?"

Again there was silence. Beth's death was not a subject he discussed with anybody, ever. But eight years was a long time. He'd stopped hurting, he realized, long ago. Even so . . . "It doesn't matter," he said.

"It matters if it's coming between us. You don't talk about yourself, Rob. How can I get to know you if you won't talk?"

You can't get to know me, that's just it. I'm a special agent, here on an assignment. I can't let anybody close to me.

"Look, Cat, I don't talk, and I can't love. So we'd better just be sensible and forget it, hadn't we?"

"You're afraid, aren't you? You've had losses in your life that you won't even talk about, much less accept. You can't get close to anyone because it might mean losing again."

"I thought that was your problem," he said tightly.

"Maybe you've got it even worse than I do."

He started to argue, but the words caught in his throat. Could it be that he was using his job as an excuse? Even Beth had complained that he didn't open up enough, that he built walls around himself that nobody could penetrate. Was it true? And if so, why? He thought briefly of his childhood, posted with his diplomat parents from one troubled country to the next. Painfully making new friends—for he'd been shy—only to lose them a few months later when the next move came. His mother's death, when he was twelve, of cancer. And never getting close to his father, who also hadn't been able to talk about his job.

He closed his eyes. Cat was right. It wasn't *her* inability to trust that was keeping them apart. It was her caution, based on the intuitive knowledge that he wouldn't be able to match her in feeling, emotion, perhaps not even in passion. She was a child of fire, a child of light. He walked in darkness—the kind of coldness that could quench her flames forever.

Once again he was reminded how wrong it would be to pursue her. He shouldn't have called. He should have had the will—and the kindness—to leave her alone.

"Rob?"

"What?"

Cat hesitated, then said, "I have this strong urge to take a chance on you, in spite of everything I know—or rather, don't know—about you. Is that invitation for tomorrow still open?"

Oh, God! The savage joy that leapt through him at the possibility of her saying yes almost undid him. He wanted to toss his good resolutions to the winds. He wanted to take her, crush her in his arms, and make love to her until he collapsed with exhaustion. He certainly didn't want to entertain any silly moral qualms.

He could hardly believe it was his own voice that answered, "If you're generous enough to offer, I can be generous enough to refuse. No, sweetheart. You've been right all along. I'd only hurt you—very badly, I'm beginning to think. I'm going to hang up now. Good-bye."

"The trouble is, I think I'm a little in love with you already," she said very quietly.

Rob broke the connection, pretending not to hear. Then he lay awake all night while her words danced endlessly through his brain, tempting him, luring him, giving him hope, and filling him with guilt.

CHAPTER SEVEN

THE FOLLOWING NIGHT, Rob offered to help Emma with the cameras and telescope in the observatory. Why not? He wasn't getting any sleep, anyway. And although the elderly astronomer didn't admit it, she was clearly getting a little too frail for some of the heavier tasks involved in viewing the stars.

"These damn steps are the worst part of the job," she panted as she and Rob climbed the long metal staircase to the dome at ten in the evening to begin the "day's" work. "They may kill me yet."

He could see why. The stairs were brutal, even for a man of his strength and conditioning, yet, Emma had to be somewhere between seventy and eighty years old.

Until tonight, Rob had avoided working with Emma because he didn't want to reveal himself to be behind the times in his knowledge of what was happening in the world of astronomy. So far, however, Emma had demonstrated little curiosity about his work. She had been told that he was interested in the possibility of communicating with intelligent life in other solar systems but that he was skeptical about Aberdeen Island's UFO's.

As they opened the great sliding panels to the depths of the night, positioned the sixty-inch reflector, and readied the photographic plates for tonight's exposures, Rob felt a pang of nostalgia. What would have happened if he hadn't quit stargazing himself? Would he have made any significant contribution to science, come up with any brilliant insights into the creation of the universe, the myriad mysteries of the cosmos? Discovered a comet, perhaps, or a black hole? Charted the course of a legitimate UFO?

He frowned. Astronomy, he reminded himself, was a killing, thankless discipline. You craned your neck for hours, staring through a telescope, or, more frequently, at a bunch of photographic plates, trying to detect sights and sounds that were all but imperceptible. It was boring, lonely, impossible. It played havoc with one's sleep cycle, not to mention one's sex life. If one was lucky enough to have a sex life.

Cat, Cat. He kept remembering her final, quiet remark on the phone last night. *I think I'm a little in love with you already.* Why did the memory of those words make his mouth go dry and his throat begin to ache? Did he want a woman's love? This woman's love?

"How much longer are you going to be here, Rob?" Emma interrupted his thoughts to ask.

"Until I get the evidence I need," he said grimly.

"Evidence?" she repeated, giving him an odd look.

"I'd like to see one of these so-called UFO's," he clarified.

"Well, I appreciate your helping me tonight," she went on as she got ready to study the photographic plates from the night before. "But if you really want some evidence

of UFO's, you'd best make your way over to the far side
of the island."

Rob had already determined that the opposite side of
the island, the side where he and Cat had had their picnic,
was the vicinity where most of the strange lights had
been seen. It had been there that he'd concentrated his
search for illegal weapons. He'd found nothing so far,
but he hadn't really expected to. According to Morton,
the latest shipment was still being assembled on the mainland, but one of these nights David Kineer and his smuggler friends would load the guns into a couple of small
boats and move them to Aberdeen Island, where they
would transfer their weapons to a rogue pilot who would
fly them out of the country.

What he didn't know was whether this would all happen on the same night, or whether the smugglers had a
place on the island to hole up for a day or two with their
contraband. He suspected the latter, but despite his careful searching, he had been unsuccessful in discovering
their hideout.

"What do you think the lights are, Emma?" he asked.

If he expected a rational answer from a fellow scientist, Rob was disappointed. "Most of them are nothing
but islanders' drunken visions, but a few, I imagine, are
real enough."

He raised his eyebrows. "Real enough what?"

"Vestiges of another world, perhaps? Glimmerings of
a parallel universe? Signs and portents seeping through
from the future or the past? Who knows?"

Rob stared. "Are you serious?"

The elderly astronomer smiled and patted his hand
comfortingly. "Take heart. When I was your age, I would
have sniggered, too. But forty years of gazing out into
space has taught me to take nothing for granted, particularly our knowledge of what's possible in the physical
universe. Duncan MacFarlane is not as crazy as he seems."

Rob made a deprecatory noise, which Emma ignored.

"His explanation—Project Earth—is a little too facile, but he's right, I think, about the universe being an illusion. Look up there." She pointed into the cloak of darkness above them, pricked as it was by the twinkling of a thousand million stars. "You're looking, as you know full well, into the past. Depending upon which star you focus on, you're seeing eleven years into the past, twenty-seven years into the past, two thousand years into the past, or—with those new computer-operated multifaced reflectors they're building on that volcano in Hawaii—millions of years into the past. The familiar configuration of the night sky is illusory itself. How many of those stars have burned themselves out long before their light reaches our telescopes?"

"That doesn't make the stars any less real," he argued. "We don't know what they're like today, although we can make some pretty accurate projections. But we know what they were like eleven, twenty-seven, two thousand, or a million years ago."

"It's all one," she said a little vaguely. "The past, the future, the birth and death of galaxies, the mellowing of the human heart."

This island, thought Rob, is full of weirdos.

"Do you like Cat MacFarlane?" the old woman asked.

He made a less-than-brilliant effort to control his surprise. "I've only met the woman a couple of times."

"I've known her since she was little," Emma went on. She shot Rob an appraising glance. "Nice girl."

"Much too nice for the likes of me," Rob growled.

"Of course, you're a Hepburn."

He raised his eyebrows. "You know about the Hepburn-MacFarlane clan feud?"

"Duncan told me all about it this afternoon. Complained to me that you'd been romancing his granddaughter and made sure I understood how unsuitable it was." She cracked a smile. "As if *I* had any say in the matter."

"I haven't been romancing his granddaughter."

"Duncan will come around eventually, of course," she went on as if he hadn't spoken. "Particularly if the prophecy were to come true."

Rob couldn't resist. "What prophecy?"

"It seems it was decreed back in Scotland hundreds of years ago that the MacFarlanes would hate the Hepburns until the day when—what was it?—the waters burn, the caverns sing, and the sun showers its glory at midnight."

"The Day of Judgment," he translated.

"You never know with prophecy," said Emma. She paused a moment, then added, "I'm very fond of Cat MacFarlane. I wouldn't want to see her hurt."

Good God, Cat certainly didn't lack protectors! "Neither would I."

"It strikes me, Rob, that I really don't know very much about you," Emma persisted.

"I'm not seeing Cat MacFarlane," Rob said dryly, "so you and her grandfather can quit worrying."

The words were no sooner out of his mouth when the phone rang. Emma picked up the receiver on the computer console, listened a moment, then held it out to Rob. "It's for you," she said with a perfectly straight face. "It's Cat."

"I'll take it downstairs," Rob choked and escaped.

He was down the long stairway and into the living area in record time. He snatched up the phone. "Cat?"

"Rob? I'm so glad I got you. I thought you might be out somewhere."

He heard the urgent note in her voice. "What's the matter?"

"Rob, I think I just saw a UFO. Lights, anyway, bright. Coming in low and making a strange, almost musical sound."

He sucked in his breath. "Where?"

"Out by the old airstrip I took you to the other day.

It—whatever it was—appeared to be landing."

He muttered an expletive. The boats bearing the gun runners ought to have arrived before the plane. And there had been no word from Morton. "Okay. I'm going to check it out."

"I'll meet you there."

"No!" He adjusted the tone of his voice and repeated, "No, I'd rather you didn't. Just stay home."

"But, Rob, I want to know what it is. It's my first UFO, after all."

"Look, Cathy, it may be dangerous. Just stay in the castle, please? If there's nothing threatening, I'll come and fetch you, I promise. Okay?"

"My grandfather won't let you in."

"Then meet me out front, for godsake! Cat. I've got to go. I'll talk to you later."

She stopped arguing. "Be careful, Rob," she said huskily.

"Always." He replaced the phone, stared at it for a moment, then unlocked the closet where he kept his private telecommunicator. Speaking in Agency code, he got through to Morton, who told him that as far as anybody on that end knew, the guns had not yet been shifted to Aberdeen Island. He broke the connection, puzzled. Of course, Morton could be wrong. He yelled up to Emma that he was going out for a while.

"Have a nice time," she called back, her voice echoing loudly through the dome-roofed building. Jeez, the acoustics were terrific, he realized. The old lady had probably heard every word he'd said, Agency code and all.

Annoyed by his carelessness, he slammed the door of his one-room flat, still trying to make sense of Cat's sighting. Either the pilot was making a dry run, or somebody else was using the old runway on the MacFarlane property.

As he slipped his arms into a dark concealing jacket,

he didn't even consider a third possibility: that Cat MacFarlane was lying to him.

Cat put down the phone by her bed, went to the mirror, and stared at the combined excitement, apprehension, and guilt in her eyes. It had worked—he was coming. She lifted her thick hair off her shoulders for a second, then let it fall free. It looked redder than ever against the pale green gossamer dress she'd chosen. Sleeveless and a little lower in the bosom than she normally wore, the ankle-length summer gown was one of her stage costumes. It made her look fragile and ethereal, except for her hair, which, like her body, was aflame.

She'd been agonizing over this decision ever since her conversation with Rob last night. Now that it was made, she felt a certain relief. Relief, along with hot, sweet anticipation.

She was going to make love to Rob. Despite his qualms and her own. She was going to seduce him, if need be. For one night she was going to be the alluring Siren he'd compared her to. One night. And afterward? Don't even think about *afterward,* she instructed herself.

She knew she was being foolish. She had little in common with this rational, skeptical man who could so calmly deny his ability to love. He couldn't open up to her, and he wasn't interested in taking any emotional risks. There was no doubt about it: He would hurt her.

But even so, the emptiness of Rob Hepburn's life had touched Cat's heart as much as his dark sensuality had touched her body. She wanted to give him something, something with no strings attached. She wanted to share with him the illusions he denigrated—lend him some of her music, her poetry, the ineffable things that enrich the soul. For she sensed there was something in him that was worth reaching out to. There was a warm and caring man somewhere in there behind his walls. She knew it from his humor, his tolerance of her grandfather, his tender, considerate way of making love.

One night. It would undoubtedly mean far more to her than it would mean to him, but at least she knew what to expect this time. At least there were no lies between them. She knew Rob wouldn't be making the kind of commitment to her that Josh had pretended to make. Rob had been honest; she had no hopes for a long-term relationship. It didn't matter; for the first time in her life she was willing to give herself without them.

Cat touched a little perfume to the gold chain at her throat, then frowned at herself. As usual, her reflection didn't send her soaring into ecstasies of self-admiration. There was too much red in her hair—although Rob didn't seem to mind that; her turned-up nose was too cute, her mouth too wide. Some Siren! Placing her hands on her hips, she sucked in her stomach and thrust out her breasts, then burst out laughing at the artificial nature of her pose. "You really want this body, Hepburn?" she said out loud. "You must be as balmy as your ancestors."

Sticking her tongue out at the mirror, she turned and hurried outside to meet him.

Rob would approach the old runway via the coast road, Cat expected. It was the way they had come the day of the picnic, the only way he knew. She herself was coming from the opposite direction—down the slope in back of her grandfather's castle, through the flower gardens she'd planted, under a grape arbor, and down a winding path that led through a forest of dense pines. The woods covered the hill to the left of the airstrip; Rob would come over the hill to the right. It was there, at the summit of that last hill, that she planned to wait for him.

There was only a half moon that night, but it was high and very bright. There was a warm breeze, and the stars were dancing. Cat ran lightly along the pine-needled path, humming to herself as she went. When she reached the hilltop, she settled down against a rock and began to sing.

Rob approached the landing site in a very different frame of mind. Tense and alert, the adrenaline flowing through his system, he was ready for violence, not love. But he came over the hill from the coast road stealthily, silent as a shadow. If the smuggler's pilot was making a dry run tonight, the last thing he wanted to do was scare him away. The quarry was to be flushed when the contraband was on them, and not before.

The wind was blowing from off the water behind him, and it would bear his sounds before him if he was not careful. It meant he heard nothing from the landing strip until he was almost upon it. Nor did he see any lights.

Rob crouched in the shadow of a tall pine as he crested the hill and surveyed the valley below. It was after eleven, but the moon lit the runway clearly. There was nothing there. Experienced eyes ran over the entire area, alert for the slightest motion. There was nothing anywhere.

He cursed softly even as he acknowledged that this was exactly what he ought to have expected. If the pilot had been reconnoitering here tonight and trying a practice landing, he certainly wouldn't have stuck around for any length of time afterward. He'd have checked out the strip, then got his ass off it as quickly as possible.

Still moving carefully, Rob descended into the valley. Aberdeen Castle was somewhere over the next rise and through the woods, and Cat would be waiting there to hear his report. He couldn't think of a better excuse than that to go to her.

Just then the wind shifted, and he heard the singing. He stopped dead, listening. The breeze distorted the sound, and it was an instant before Rob understood. He remembered Cat's description of bright lights and strange musical sounds. And Emma's assertion that some of the UFO's were real. He shivered slightly, touched by a profound, atavistic, and totally irrational fear of all the things that were beyond human knowing. Things whose existence he, in a more normal state of mind, would have considered laughable and absurd. And then the wind shifted again, bringing the sounds more clearly to his ears, and he knew the clear, sweet notes for what they were.

He started up the hill at a run, furious with her for disobeying his order to stay safely at the castle. When he reached the summit, there was no sign of her. "Cat?" he called, his adrenaline pumping. "Where the hell are you, dammit?"

Her song—and her laughter—continued from deep in the pine forest. Magical notes . . . luring him after her. Sensual notes, teasing subtly, promising. A Siren's song. His anger changed to surprise, then to hot, heady excitement as it occurred to him that there had been no airplane, no strange lights, no UFO. She'd tricked him, beguiled him. She'd lured him out here for another purpose entirely.

"Cat MacFarlane, you disobeyed my orders," he called after her. "I told you to stay at the castle. D'you know what happens to headstrong women who dare to be so bold?"

Her answer was a soft, musical laugh. He could see her now, running lightly ahead of him, her slender form cloaked in a diaphanous faerie gown, her fiery hair drifting over her bare upper arms. "What happens, Hepburn?"

"The same thing that happened to your female ancestors, lady."

"You'll have to catch me first," she trilled back at him.

"Oh, I'll catch you. You can count on that."

"I am counting on it," she laughed, but she continued to flee.

Rob's blood began to pound in fierce exultation. He paced her, not overtaking her yet, even though it would take very little extra effort to do so. Slowly, now. Not too soon. He was intoxicated by her lure, her song, the joy of the chase. His former qualms were forgotten. This time the end was not in doubt. This time, at last, the hunter would bring his quarry down.

"Siren," he whispered, letting the wind take his words to her. "Your voice is full of promises. Will you keep them?"

Her song burst over him, music so achingly beautiful that the lyrics hardly mattered. Her *yes* was there in the melody even more clearly than in the words.

"Cat?" he called gently a few moments later. He couldn't see her, although her music was very near. "Where are you leading me?"

Her voice fluttered briefly, then returned:

> "My highland love, where art thou roaming?
> Remember, sweet, our nights of loving?
> Oh, come thee soon again?"

It was the song she'd sung on the night they'd met. She'd stopped running, he realized; her music no longer retreated. They were in a grove of pines, sheltered from all but the whispers of the wind. He slowed till he was barely moving, approaching her silently as she sang a verse he didn't remember:

> "I love thee true, my heart's own flower,
> Come lie with me within my bower,
> I'll yield to thee, tonight!"

She was there, before him, half turned away, her hair rising with the air currents and licking flames around her. He closed the distance between them and caught a strand of it between his fingers. He raised it to his lips.

"Cathy," he murmured, hardly daring to take her in his arms lest his mortal flesh disturb her Siren song.

She turned, smiling, her eyes alight with tenderness and excitement, her body as feminine and alluring as Eve's. One hand came up and gently touched his cheek. "Hello, astronomer," she said.

His hands fell to her shoulders, then moved up into the soft, thick mass of her hair. "Bright lights?" he said, trying to assume an austere expression. "Strange musical sounds? You have no idea, woman, of the trouble you caused tonight with your wild and improbable tales."

"I'll make it up to you."

"Mmm," he agreed, sliding one hand down to the nape of her neck, which he caressed lightly with his thumb. "I intend to see that you do." The hand moved on downward, following the line of her spine all the way to its end. He felt her shiver; he shivered, too, and his breath came out raggedly. She moved closer just as he was about to jerk her violently into his arms. She came to him, wrapped her arms around him, and lifted her mouth for his kiss.

He held back for only a moment. "Sweetheart, are you sure? Once I begin, there'll be no stopping me, so be sure, Cat. Be very sure."

"I am sure," she whispered.

"But nothing's changed," he insisted. "You understand that, don't you?" His voice was anguished as he repeated, "For godsake, nothing's changed."

She smiled serenely. "One thing has, Rob. My mind."

He read the truth of that in her eyes. He didn't understand it, but it was beyond him to question her further. Everything was beyond him now, except her light, her fire, her song. With a sigh of surrender, he bent his head to take her soft, sweet lips.

CHAPTER EIGHT

CAT KNEW AS soon as he touched her that this was going to be special, very special. But even so she wasn't prepared for the sweetness that stole through her when Rob's mouth moved on hers. Passion was there, of course, burning brightly, hotly, but the sweetness was something of another order. It confirmed that there was more to this man than he had let her see so far.

He was very gentle with her. Although she could feel his hard muscles trembling with desire, he didn't rush her. Instead of jamming her against him, he stroked her seductively, allowing her to decide when and how to fit her body to his. There was no teasing to his actions, just care and a respect for her own pacing that touched her deeply. He was not a selfish lover—but she knew that already. That afternoon in the cave, it had been her pleasure he had courted rather than his own.

But when she did move in close enough to feel the imprint of his hips, his thighs, his rampant arousal, a shudder went through him and his gentle kiss turned masterful. Suddenly she felt his tongue, his teeth. Suddenly his hands were moving on her, claiming every inch of her flesh as his to explore. Suddenly he was the fierce Hepburn warrior, and she the trembling MacFarlane lady. And it was exciting, transporting, wonderful!

He raised his head enough for her to see his desire-darkened eyes, his arrogant blade of a nose, his harsh yet sensual mouth. His cheeks and chin were rough, unshaven. For an instant she imagined what that sandpapery skin would feel like against her bare breasts, and the resulting knot of lust that twisted inside her made her gasp.

"What?" he whispered.

Her eyelids fluttered closed, and her spirit soared free, abandoned, shameless. "I want to feel you against me," she murmured. "Here." Her fingers flew to the bodice of her dress, where a dozen tiny buttons ran from her throat to her waist. She undid the first two, then felt his hands closing over hers, helping her. Together they dispensed with the buttons, and the bodice parted, exposing her unbound breasts to the moon, the night wind, and Rob's eyes.

"You're beautiful," he told her, reverently touching one creamy breast and then the other. "What's in here?" he asked, putting his finger on the gold locket that was the only jewelry adorning her. "You always wear it—does it hold a picture?"

"It's empty. My grandmother used to have a picture of herself and Granddad, and someday I'll have a picture of myself and—" She stopped.

"Your husband?"

"My true love, whoever he may be," she finished. "I wear it as a good luck charm. My grandmother once told me it would protect me in times of danger. I know that's crazy and superstitious, but still, I never take it off."

"Silly," he said affectionately. His thumb grazed the rosy brown tip of her breast, retreated, then touched it again, almost by accident. Both nipples hardened in anguish, longing for him, but his touches continued to be moth-light and elusive. Cat moaned while he tantalized her; her knees went weak, and she would have slipped to the ground were it not for the support of his other arm around her waist.

"What?" he asked again, mischievously this time.

"You're tormenting me!"

"Ah, but you're the Siren. I have to be very careful. For centuries you've been luring men with your song, drawing the very life out of them until nothing but their bones remain."

"Poor Sirens. Better a live man than a pile of bones! Didn't anybody ever survive?"

"Two men did. Ulysses was one of them."

"I remember that story. He had his sailors stop their ears with wax when they sailed past the Sirens' island, but he left his own ears open."

"Only after taking the precaution of binding himself tightly to the ship's mast. He heard the Sirens' summons, but he was powerless to obey it. It nearly drove him mad."

"Yes, I remember. But who was the other man who heard the Sirens and escaped?"

"Orpheus. The lyrical musician whose song was even more spellbinding than the Sirens' own. When they sang for him, he simply made his own music, and they couldn't touch him. A sort of musical duel, I imagine." He smiled, his eyes hot with sensual promises. "I can't make music, Siren, but like Orpheus, I intend to weave a spell around you all the same."

She ran her fingers under the hem of his dark T-shirt and up over the supple muscles of his chest. "Is this a duel, then?" she asked huskily.

He let go of her long enough to strip the shirt over his head. At the same time he kicked off his shoes and stood before her, tall, virile, and magnificent, clad only in tight black jeans, looking as lithe and potent as anything the Greeks had to offer. "Winner take all," he agreed.

Greedy now, Cat's fingers fell to the fastening of his jeans. She wanted to see him naked, to feel the hard thrust of his desire under her eager hands. He allowed her to minister to him, his body tense with self-imposed control as she slid down his zipper and tugged together on his jeans and his briefs.

They slid down his legs, and he kicked them off, groaning as Cat's hands lovingly explored him, teasing him as effectively as he had teased her breasts. Her light fingers stroked up and down his aroused length, caressed his hair-sprung legs and thighs, came back, hovered, touched him once, then fluttered away, only to come back and touch him far too briefly again...

"God!" he muttered. He seized her wrists and forced her hands against him. She laughed, resisting, and the musical tones of her laughter did him in. Control gone, he jerked her close and kissed her ravenously, then tore at the fragile cloth that separated his flesh from hers. Somehow he stripped the dress off her without ripping it to shreds, then toppled her onto the bed of pine needles covering the ground.

Her panties he dispensed with just as ruthlessly, and they were naked together beneath the stars. Rob's gaze wandered over her slim silken body; he forced himself to be gentle as he swept his hands from her breasts to her thighs and back. He dipped his head and lightly tongued a velvet-peaked nipple. Cat crooned deep in her throat and parted her thighs, urging him down upon her.

"Sweetheart..." His voice was tense as he slid between her legs; Cat could feel the dampness of his skin, the humid heat of his breath against her mouth. "I can't hold back."

"Don't. Don't hold back, Rob."

"I'll hurt you. I haven't fully prepared you."

She arched her lower body against him so he could feel the moist evidence of her arousal. "I've been ready for this since the night we met," she confessed.

"Oh, love . . ." It was enough to blast whatever tenuous hold he still had on restraint. Shutting his eyes, Rob surged against her, feeling her body subtly shift to accommodate him. Then he was inside her, hotly surrounded by her smooth, tight flesh. He groaned, dazzled by the incredible pleasure that licked through him. This was different, he realized, awed. They fit together in some strange, indefinable way that he couldn't remember ever having experienced before. It was almost as if he were finding a part of himself that had been separated from him until now.

Cat, too, was dazzled. From the moment they merged she knew she loved this man—his body, his rationalistic brain, his deeply buried soul. She was his; there was no help for it. His claim on her was sexual, but she knew instinctively that in their case sex was a powerful, mystical force.

He raised his head and smiled at her. For a few moments he was still, sliding one hand between his flesh and hers to lightly trace her breasts, her sides, her hipbones, and the downy curls where they were joined. Impatient, she arched, bringing him more deeply inside her. His eyes flickered shut, and he began the smooth, slow motions of love.

"Yes, oh, yes," she murmured as she caught his rhythm effortlessly, then varied it. His dark eyes opened, smoldering. "A duel," he reminded her, then thrust deep, making her cry out. And again. Taking up his challenge, she used her muscles to clasp him even more tightly and laughed breathlessly at the sounds this wrung from him.

"Siren," he muttered. He withdrew, then wickedly, with maddening control, he slowly filled her again. At the same time his fingers teased her breasts, doubling, tripling her pleasure. Oh, heavens! His mouth came down on hers, his tongue driving deep, its rhythm an erotic counterpoint to the driving power of his hips. His rhythm was his song—more joyfully primitive than the beating of a jungle drum, and much more bewitching. Cat felt the earth tilt as she conceded him the sensual duel. Helpless, enraptured, she let him propel her through the shimmering portals of release.

But this time, unlike that afternoon in the cave, they made the journey together. Rob was with her, his cries echoing her own, his body shuddering and trembling with the same delicious convulsions that she experienced. Together they nursed their pleasure, prolonged it, let it slowly unwind around them. Their kisses and caresses continued, lightly now, gently, as they helped each other reenter the everyday world.

For a while they lay without moving, still intimately joined, sated, relaxed. Gradually Cat became aware of the night wind, which no longer seemed quite so warm on their overheated bodies. She shivered slightly. Rob felt it, rolled them both to a sitting position, and began searching for their clothes.

"So far I've made love to you on a rocky cavern floor and a carpet of pine needles. Do you suppose we could manage a bed next time?"

"This is romantic," she protested.

He slapped her lightly on the backside. "We may just end up with mosquito bites in some very unlikely places."

"There's too much breeze for mosquitoes."

"A little breeze wouldn't deter me if I were a mosquito." He nipped her shoulder. "Not with such a luscious morsel on the menu. Come on, put your dress back on. You'll catch cold. I can feel the goose bumps rising on your skin."

Regretfully they both dressed; then Rob began to walk her in the direction of the castle. He held her close against his hip; her hair fluttered against his throat. Neither spoke, but the silence was companionable.

When they reached the garden behind the castle and looked up at the daunting stone walls atop the rise ahead of them, Rob said, "Maybe you, your grandfather, and Emma are right that time is an illusion. Space, too, for that matter. Look at that. Are we here on U.S. soil in the twentieth century, or back in Scotland in the fifteenth?"

"I don't know. Maybe it really doesn't matter. Maybe each moment lasts forever."

He turned to her and kissed her. "If that's true, I know which moment I'd choose to spend eternity in." When she raised her eyebrows quizzically, he added, "The moment when the hardhearted dame broke her number-one rule and invited me inside."

She laughed, and the sound carried. Rob put his hand over her mouth. "Hush. You'll wake the sleeping dragon."

"You mean Granddad?"

"I'll bet he'd burn me to a crisp if he found out what we've been up to."

"No doubt. There's no such thing as a good Hepburn, he insists. Oh, dear. We'll have to do something about Granddad."

"Short of bringing about the Day of Judgment, I can't imagine what."

"The Day of Judgment?"

"Apparently there's a prophecy regarding the climax of the infamous Hepburn-MacFarlane feud. Something about waters boiling and I forget what else."

"'When the waters burn, the caverns sing, and the sun showers its glory at midnight,'" she quoted. "'On that fateful day shall all hatred cease and the clans be united in love.'"

"Very apocalyptic," said Rob dryly.

"We had melodramatic ancestors," she agreed.

As they walked quietly around the side of the castle, Cat pointed out her window on the second floor. "See the light? That's my bedchamber, as Granddad archaically refers to it. Think you could scale that wall, Hepburn?"

It looked all but sheer to her, but Rob was unimpressed. "Sure," he said. "It's only about thirty feet up to your sill, and there's a first-story ledge in between."

"Are you serious?"

"O ye of little faith. I've done some rock-climbing in my day, sweetheart."

"You're a pretty strange astronomer," she said with a laugh. "I've always pictured professional stargazers as the squinting, hunched-over, decidedly unphysical type."

Rob shifted a little uneasily, wishing he could tell Cat the truth about his job. He couldn't, of course. He had no more right to violate his cover than Josh Evans had had. His eyes closed momentarily as he prayed he wouldn't hurt her the way his predecessor had. You won't, a dry voice inside him said. You'll hurt her far, far more.

In front of the castle he held her close once more. She was shivering now; the breeze had turned decidedly cool. "Tomorrow?" he suggested against his better judgment.

She nodded against his throat. For a moment she'd feared he wouldn't ask.

"Come to the observatory. Emma sleeps during the day, and I have the place to myself."

"What time?"

He kissed her long and slow. "As early as you can. Escape the dragon, and come."

"I don't want to go in," she objected, her lips clinging to his. "I want to spend the night with you."

"Well, why don't you sneak me into the castle?"

"I can't. Grandfather would never forgive me if he found out."

"I could climb in."

"You're crazy, Hepburn." She laughed, then shivered again.

"I'd keep you out all night if you weren't all goose-bumpy. Go in, sun-child." Gently he pushed her to arm's length. "The sooner you sleep, the sooner it'll be morning."

She touched his cheek in that sweet way she had. "'Night, astronomer," she whispered, then tossed him a smile and ran lightly inside.

Rob watched her go with a frown on his lips. She'd asked for nothing, he knew. But he wished he had something to give her all the same.

CHAPTER NINE

CAT HAD BEEN in bed for no more than ten minutes when she heard an odd scratching outside her window. Opening her eyes, she stared, dumbfounded, as a dark shape appeared on the ledge. The shape of a man.

She almost screamed—with fear for him. Hurling her naked limbs out of bed, she ran to the window and raised it. "You maniac! You'll break your neck!"

Rob's face was level with her breasts, a position he lost no time in taking advantage of. He rubbed against her. "But what a way to go."

"Oh, my God," she moaned, staring down at the ground as she pulled him over the windowsill. He wasn't even breathing hard, although there was a light coating of sweat on his arms. "What if you'd fallen?"

He was brushing his hands on his jeans and looking very pleased with himself. "I couldn't wait until tomorrow, after all," he informed her. "Besides, as I told your grandfather on the night we met, I can't resist a challenge."

"Don't you every try that again!"

He grinned. "Mad at me?"

"Yes!" But she was finding it difficult to persist in her disapproval. She'd wanted more time with him, and here he was.

"Come here. I want my reward." When she pretended to hesitate, standing there naked and annoyed, her hair flaming and her arms akimbo, Rob raised his eyebrows and began stalking her. "Come on, love. The Hepburn raider's here to do a little ravaging and pillaging. Mostly ravaging."

Cat backed away from him, failing to remember that the bed was right behind her. It came up against the back of her thighs, halting her retreat. "I ought to scream, as my ancestors would have. My grandfather would wake up and come running, and we'd see firsthand if you're as good at exits as you are at entrances."

"You're not going to scream, and your precious ancestors probably didn't either. I'll bet every last one of them went willingly into her ravisher's arms."

"Chauvinistic wretch!" she laughed as he halted his advance to strip off his clothes. Excitement swept through her as his uncompromisingly male form emerged from his shirt and jeans. She collapsed into the bed and pulled the sheet over her body as she stared happily at his. "On second thought, Hepburn, if the ravishers looked anything like you, you're probably right about that."

"I think you just paid me a compliment."

"Come to bed, and I'll pay you a few more."

"Is your bedroom door locked?"

"Yes, it is, but you might lower your voice a little. The room isn't soundproof, you know!"

"Then you'll just have to try to contain your cries of ecstasy, my sweet," he whispered as he slid into bed beside her.

* * *

Cat awakened early the next morning, drifting slowly up to consciousness from a pleasant state of deep, sensual dreaming. For a moment she had no idea what that delicious warmth against her spine was; then, with a start, she remembered everything. After keeping her up for hours in a dazzling display of tender aggression, Rob had finally curled his body around hers and slept. "I'll just close my eyes for a minute or two, then sneak out of here before the castle comes to life," he'd told her. "I'll be gone long before the noble laird takes his morning tea."

Uh-oh. Cat twisted her head to see the clock. Seven-fifteen. She usually slept later, but her grandfather was up every morning by six-thirty or seven.

"Rob?" she whispered. With difficulty she extricated herself from his embrace and shook him. "Rob!"

He came awake in an instant, his entire body tensing, although he didn't move. His brown eyes opened, showing full alertness, even though she could have sworn he'd been deeply asleep moments before. Odd. The only other person she'd ever known who came awake so quickly and so completely was Josh Evans. She'd realized later it was one of the side effects of his job.

"Rob, you have to go," she told him. "My grandfather's probably already up, and if he catches you . . ."

Rob muttered an expletive, then grinned. He wiped a swath of dark hair out of his eyes and ran an incorrigible hand over her flank. "Okay, but first, as long as I'm here . . ."

"Rob, for heaven's sake!" She no sooner spoke than they heard footsteps outside in the hall. "Oh, my God, maybe that's him!"

"Does he usually barge in on you at seven in the morning?"

"No, but—"

"And you said your door was locked, right?"

"Uh-huh."

The footsteps seemed to be coming closer. "It's probably one of the staff," Rob whispered. "You do have a staff in a huge place like this, I presume?"

"There's a housekeeper, yes. Mrs. Baldwin. And a sort of handy-man-gardener named Joe. But that was Granddad—I know the way he walks." She looked wildly around the room. Large and airy, it didn't provide much in the way of cover. "Get under the bed," she ordered him.

"I'm not getting under the damn bed!"

"You have to!"

"This is ridiculous, Cat; you're acting paranoid. You're an adult; you have a lover. Even if it *is* your grandfather, and even if he does try to barge in, I'm certainly not going to cower in front of the man."

"You're a Hepburn," she moaned. "If he doesn't try to murder you for compromising my honor, it'll only be because he's too busy collapsing of apoplexy. Rob! He's seventy-five years old! He's old-fashioned. Get under the bed."

Rob swore violently. He'd been in some damnable situations in his life, but this was absurd. He had never hidden under a woman's bed, and he wasn't about to start now. If her damn grandfather had objections to their affair, let him state them to his face. He certainly wasn't going to hide from the consequences of his actions like some weaselly coward.

On the other hand, Cat was giving him the sort of imploring look that he found irresistible. She was embarrassed, he realized. Apprehensive, too.

For once in his life Rob decided his machismo wasn't everything. He'd gotten her into this predicament, after all. If he hadn't been so hot for her last night, he wouldn't have climbed the blasted wall.

"I'll get you for this," he muttered as he slid out the far side of the bed and under the frilly ruff that edged the antique bedstead. The footsteps, meanwhile, approached the door, hesitated briefly, then stopped altogether. Moments later there was a sharp rap on the door.

Cat was about to call out a sleepy "Who is it?" when she saw Rob's T-shirt, jeans, and sneakers lying in a pile on the floor, smack between the bed and the door. Good Lord! Leaping out of bed, she threw a robe around her and grabbed up the clothes. The knock was repeated. "Yes, what is it?" she called back in a sleepy voice as she shoved Rob's things under the ruff, kicking up a cloud of dust as she did so. He choked, then sneezed then cursed softly.

"You just failed Housekeeping 101, woman," he hissed. "Don't you ever mop under the damn bed?"

"Shut *up!*" she whispered.

"Cat?" her grandfather called. "Are you awake in there?"

"Not really," she yelled back. "What do you want at this hour?"

"Open the door, Cat," he said in a stern, uncompromising tone. "Mrs. Baldwin says there's something funny going on around here, and I want to know what it is."

Oh, dear. "I'll be right there," she called back, adding in a whisper to Rob, "And don't sneeze!" as she moved to unlock the door.

When he heard the key turn, Duncan MacFarlane flung open the door and stared suspiciously while Cat tried her best not to look as guilty as she felt. The bed was a tousled confusion of untucked sheets and rumpled pillows—she'd have had to suffer nightmares all night long to make such a wreck of the bed by herself. And her face was red with beard-burn, her lips bruised with too much kissing.

"Are you sick?" he asked her, staring at her flushed face.

"No, but I couldn't sleep last night. I tossed and turned till morning. Now what's this about something funny going on? Don't tell me sensible old Mrs. Baldwin has finally seen a UFO?"

"Mrs. Baldwin couldn't sleep last night either," he informed her. Cat noted that his eyes were shifting, looking surreptitiously into every corner of the room. "She got up in the middle of the night to go downstairs for a glass of hot milk, and she reports that she heard voices out in the garden. A woman's voice *and* a man's.

Cat stared at the way her grandfather's chin was jutting out. Inadvertently she smiled. "Why do I get the feeling I'm being accused of some enormous moral indiscretion?" she asked. "Am I supposed to confess that it was me in the garden last night?"

"Was it?"

"Yes, as a matter of fact. I couldn't sleep. Like Mrs. Baldwin, I strolled around instead. So what?"

"Who was the man?" he growled. He was looking around openly now, but fortunately Rob was well hidden—and controlling his reaction to her failed housekeeping, so far, at least. "And where is he now?"

She didn't have any difficulty affecting anger, since she was beginning to feel rather a lot of it. "Take a good look around, Grandfather," she said in a scathing voice. She only called him Grandfather when she was mad. "Do you want to try the closet? Behind the curtains? Under the bed?"

"I wouldn't put it past that slimy Hepburn fellow to be hiding in a corner with his tail between his legs!" her grandfather roared.

Uh-oh. Cat felt the surge of Rob's anger as strongly as if their minds were linked. She'd kill him if he was about to erupt out of there, naked and enraged. She recalled the defiant way he'd kissed her that first night in front of Granddad. Don't you dare, she warned him mentally.

"You have a helluva nerve, Grandfather! I can't believe you're actually standing there accusing me of—of I don't know what!"

Duncan MacFarlane was beginning to seem a trifle abashed. "I know you're a woman grown, Catherine," he said in a more conciliatory tone. "You're a lovely woman, too, who deserves a man, a *good* man, lassie. Not a sly, seducing blackguard like Robert Hepburn."

"You're passing judgment on a man you know nothing about. It's not fair to do that, Granddad. You, of all people, who always taught me how important it was to be tolerant and fair—how can you act this way?"

"I know one thing about him," her grandfather said sullenly. "He's not an astronomer."

"What do you mean, he's not an astronomer? Of course he's an astronomer. He's here to investigate the UFO's."

"He doesn't *look* like an astronomer," her grandfather insisted. "He looks like a Hepburn warlord."

"Really, Granddad, your obsession with this clan feud is beginning to worry me!"

Duncan MacFarlane sighed. "It's your happiness I'm obsessed with, girl."

Cat made an effort to swallow her anger. She threw him a tentative smile. "I know that, Granddad, and I appreciate it. But when it comes to men, I can take care of myself, okay? I don't need to be watched and guarded like a medieval virgin. I'm going to say the same thing to Mrs. Baldwin as soon as I get downstairs. My love affairs are no one's business but my own."

"I just wish you'd find a nice man, marry, and settle down with him."

"I'm afraid that's not very likely," she returned, wishing Rob Hepburn were not overhearing all this.

"No," MacFarlane said unhappily. He sighed. "There was another sighting last night."

"There was?" Thank God! Maybe it would get his mind off the subject of nice men and marriage.

"Another globe of light, apparently playing music, out over the water on the eastern side of the island."

"Who saw it?"

"Jon Hayden."

"Again?" Maybe Hayden was a drinker, after all.

"Lucky, isn't he?" her grandfather said wistfully. He ran a hand over his brow, looking tired suddenly, and old. "I'm sorry, Cat," he said slowly. "With Jon blathering about lights, and Mrs. Baldwin hearing strange voices and claiming she'd seen a vampire climbing up the castle wall—"

"What?!"

"Didn't I tell you? She looked out from the kitchen— you can see this wing from there, you know—and she thought she saw a shadowy batlike figure crawling up the castle wall. Like they do, you know, in those Dracula movies."

Cat couldn't help herself. She began to laugh. She laughed so hard her face turned a color that competed with the red in her hair. Duncan MacFarlane, watching her, began to smile, too, and very faintly, Cat heard a sound that sounded as though the occupant of the dust-trap under her bed was losing his grip on control.

Hurriedly taking her grandfather by the arm, she walked him toward the door. "So you and Mrs. Baldwin have been wondering if I was up here in bed having my neck bitten?" she asked.

"I may be old and eccentric, but I still have the wit to know that if anybody was biting your neck, 'twould be a man, not a vampire!" her grandfather retorted.

Cat was still laughing. "It was a vampire, Granddad," she said, raising her arms and snapping imaginary fangs at him. "He's converted me, so you'd better run before I come seeking you and Mrs. Baldwin as my next victims!"

Looking a little ashamed of the trouble he'd caused, her grandfather turned on his heel and left.

"You can come out now, Drac," Cat said softly as her grandfather's footsteps faded away down the hall. She closed the door firmly and locked it.

Rob slid out on his stomach, accompanied by his clothes, a slipper, a paperback mystery by Stephen Silkwood, a high-heeled designer shoe that Cat had been searching for for weeks, and numerous dust balls. He sneezed three time, then grimaced at her. "You'd better be able to cook, woman. You sure can't clean," he growled.

"Mrs. Baldwin's supposed to vacuum, but she's as lazy as I am," Cat explained, unembarrassed. "I'm sorry," she grinned, giving him a hand to help him to his feet. She brushed dust off his chin and giggled. "Thanks for doing that. I appreciate it, really."

"A vampire and a sly, seducing blackguard—Good God! You don't know how close I was to rolling out of here and slamming Grandaddy's dentures down his throat."

"Sometimes I get the feeling you are not a very nice man," she teased him.

"I'm certainly not the nice man you're supposed to settle down with and marry."

Cat met his gaze, then looked down. The mood shifted instantly; his words hurt like a slap. She remembered all that had happened during the night . . . and all that hadn't. He'd made tender, moving, exquisite love to her, but he hadn't talked. They'd held each other close and chatted in between lovemaking, yes, but it had been she who'd done most of the chatting. Rob Hepburn still hadn't revealed anything personal about himself. The few tentative questions she'd asked him he'd gently but firmly deflected. Sometimes, in the silence as he'd held her close, she'd sensed strong emotion flowing from him, felt him on the verge of dropping his guard a fraction and letting her in. But each time she'd met his eyes, hopefully, attentively, he'd caught himself, withdrawn, and held the barriers between them. How funny, she thought. He'd been the one to scale the castle walls, but she felt like the invader whose attack had to be repeatedly and strenuously rebuffed.

Don't be a jerk, she warned herself. You went into this knowing exactly what he had to offer—sensual pleasure, lots of it. No love, no commitment, no future.

Rob came up beside her, cupped her chin, and lifted it. "I'm sorry. That was a totally unnecessary remark. Forgive me?"

"Of course." She ran her fingers lightly over his knuckles and smiled.

He didn't return her smile. He stared at her flushed cheeks, her well-kissed lips, her long, slender throat. He sighed. "Last night was beautiful, Cat. You're a very warm and giving woman." His eyes and voice were absolutely serious. "Do you regret it?"

She shook her head. "Not one whit."

His eyes narrowed slightly. "Even knowing how little I had to offer you?" He waved his hand at the tousled bed. "Good though it was, it was nothing close to what you deserve."

"Rob." Her voice was soft but determined. "Don't spoil things, please."

"Your grandfather's right about one thing: You deserve a good man. A nice man. You deserve better than a sly, seducing Hepburn blackguard."

She freed her chin from his hand. "Don't!" she said sharply.

"Don't what?"

"I don't care to hear your opinions of what I *deserve*. If this is your way of making it clear to me that it's over, that you've had what you came for, that one night was enough, then just say so, Hepburn."

His mouth twisted, and his brown eyes glittered. "With you, honey, one night is nowhere near enough." He tossed his clothes on the floor again. "Get back into bed."

"Are you crazy?"

He placed his hands on her shoulders and backed her forcibly toward the bed. Cat was overwhelmed. He looked savage, dangerous, and sexy as hell.

"We can't," she whispered even as he pulled the thin robe from her slender body.

"We're going to," he countered, wrestling her down and trapping her half-resisting body beneath his. "Surrender, Cat," he whispered as his mouth and hands began to move over her. "We might not have forever, but we have today and tonight, tomorrow and the next day, and all the precious hours until I have to go." His mouth burned; his fingers played and teased, explored and parted, until she was melting in his dark and driving fire. "Yes, sweet, sweet," he said, groaning under her own gentle handling of his flesh. And at some point he added, "Love me, Cathy, love me," not knowing exactly what he said.

"I do love you, Rob," she answered. "Today and tonight, tomorrow and the next day, and all the precious hours until you have to go."

CHAPTER TEN

LATE THAT AFTERNOON Cat packed up a supper of cheese fondue and wine and loaded it into her car. Although it had been another warm and humid day, there was a heavy cloud cover, which meant that Emma would not be working tonight. This suited Cat perfectly; she intended to surprise Rob with a romantic supper, which would lead, she hoped, to more of the same pleasures they'd experienced the night before.

Driving up the road to the observatory, Cat passed Emma's cottage and saw her in her rocking chair on the front porch. Cat pulled her car over to say hello. "Don't get up," she told Emma, climbing out of the car and running lightly up the steps to the porch. Emma gave her a big smile. She was holding a big tabby cat who was purring audibly as the elderly astronomer stroked him.

"Going up to the observatory?" Emma asked.

"Yes. You're not working tonight, I presume?"

"Too cloudy. Thunderstorms are predicted for later tonight, although they say it will be fine tomorrow." She paused while Cat reached out to pat the tabby. "If you're looking for Rob Hepburn, I don't think he's there. He drove by a couple of hours ago, saying he had a UFO to investigate." Emma tilted her head to one side. "Do you know anything about a new sighting?" she asked in an odd tone.

"Yes, Jon Hayden saw something again last night, apparently. Rob's probably gone to question him. Why?"

Emma shrugged. "Nothing. It's really none of my business." She paused, then added, as if she couldn't stop herself from asking, "Are you dating him?"

"Sort of." Cat grinned. "Don't tell my grandfather, though."

"Cat, do you know anything about him?" Emma asked, sounding worried. "Where he comes from, what his background is, what, exactly, he's doing on this island?"

Cat's mental antennae instantly picked up Emma's unease. Something was wrong here. "Emma? What are you trying to tell me?"

Her old friend frowned. "I ought to be minding my own business," she clucked. "Perhaps you should just go on about yours, Catherine."

"If Rob isn't home, I've got time to kill," she said lightly. "So you might as well tell me what it is you're worried about."

"Don't misunderstand. I like the young man. He's charming, courteous, and"—her blue eyes twinkled—"very good-looking. Forty years ago I might have lost a little sleep over him myself."

Cat smiled as she rubbed behind the big cat's ears.

"I'm just not sure he's been telling us the truth, Catherine," Emma continued. "I don't think he's here to investigate UFO reports at all."

Cat felt a prickle of anxiety. *He doesn't look like an*

astronomer. "What on earth do you mean?"

"Well, the fact is, I've been a little suspicious of him from the start. A gut feeling, nothing more. But for someone who's trained as an astronomer, he has an extraordinary lack of interest in my work here."

"Maybe he's just preoccupied with his own work?"

"Maybe. When he arrived here and presented his credentials, everything certainly *looked* in order." She stopped.

"But?" Cat prodded, nervous now.

"But I'm inquisitive, that's all. And your grandfather was worried about you. So I did some checking." She paused, then went on, "Nobody's ever heard of him, Catherine. The Air Force denies him, as does NASA. No UFO-ologist, amateur or professional, is the least bit familiar with his name. It's beginning to look as though your investigator is just as mysterious as the phenomena he's supposedly here to investigate."

Cat tried to ward off a nightmarish feeling of déjà vu. Nobody had ever heard of Josh Evans, either.

"And there's something else that's odd," Emma added. "I accidently overheard part of a telephone conversation he had last night—at least, I presume it was a conversation. It was conducted in some strange foreign language I've never heard before. It may not have been a language, actually; it may have been a code."

Cat said nothing. She was beginning to feel a little sick. I'm in love with him, she was thinking. Don't let there be any reason why I shouldn't be feeling that way. "I'm sure there's some reasonable explanation," she said faintly.

Emma looked as if she wanted to believe that just as much as Cat did. "No doubt there is," she quickly agreed.

Cat looked up to the crown of the hill where the white building stood out against the dark, stormy sky. "I think I'll go on up and wait for him. And find out exactly what his explanation is."

Emma touched her hand. "Be careful, my dear."

"Be careful?"

Emma looked slightly embarrassed. "It's just an old woman's fancy, of course, but there've been moments when I've had the distinct feeling that Rob Hepburn could be a very dangerous man."

An involuntary shiver tingled over the surface of Cat's skin, but she tried to put a good face on it for Emma. "Don't worry," she said. "The Hepburns might be fierce, but the MacFarlanes are feisty. I can handle him."

But as she drove on up to the observatory, she wished she felt even a quarter as confident as she'd sounded.

It was dark when Rob returned to the observatory, dark and foggy. There would be no stargazing tonight. Which was fine with him; he'd have the place to himself. He could make his nightly contact with Morton without having to worry about being overheard by Emma. And after that was done, he could telephone Cat and invite her over for more of the spellbinding lovemaking they'd shared last night.

Walking into the darkened building, he casually flipped on a light and moved into the tiny apartment that served as his living quarters. There was a closet behind the sofa bed with a door that locked. It wasn't a sturdy lock, but it was enough to discourage any islanders who might be overly curious about his work. He withdrew the key from the pocket of his jeans and opened the closet. From a shelf in the back he removed a small computerized communications device and set its electronic power pulsing. Sitting down on the back of the sofa, facing the window that looked out on the ocean, he keyed in his code and Morton's.

"Agent Hepburn, Code Blue, Op-code seventy-seven-P," he said quietly into the transmitter, identifying himself and his assignment. Within seconds he had his superior on the other end.

"No luck finding the sea landing site yet," Rob reported somewhat tersely. "Any word on when the pigeons are going to fly?"

Possibly tonight, Morton informed him. He'd had an unconfirmed report that one of the boats might already be on the move.

"Tonight's bad," said Rob. "Lousy weather, with worse predicted. Could be too rough out there for small boats," he went on. As he spoke he shed his dark jacket, tossing it backward onto the sofa behind him. Then he loosened the shoulder holster in which he kept his .357 Magnum. He'd strapped it a little too tightly, and the leather was chafing him. The gun, too, he deposited on the sofa as he continued to speak to Morton.

Six feet behind him, crouching behind a cupboard in the kitchenette, Cat MacFarlane was staring at Rob, *Agent Hepburn,* with eyes that were misted with tears. She wanted to scream, cry, throw things. She was trembling, and her stomach was a cold lead ball. She considered herself a mild-tempered person, but if there was one thing that could rouse her to fury, this . . . *this* was it. Rob had lied to her, lied! From the beginning, just like Josh. The communicator, the shoulder holster, the gun—it was Josh all over again. She couldn't believe this was happening. It was a bad joke, a nightmare, a hallucinatory experience more bizarre than any UFO.

"You're sure about Kineer?" Rob said. "Good, I'm glad he's going to be there. This time we'll definitely nail the creep."

Cat's stomach slammed into her throat. *Kineer?* David!

"No, I'm certain about that," Rob said, apparently in answer to a question from the man on the other end. "Ms. MacFarlane's clean, no doubt about it. What d'you mean, how do I know?" He laughed suggestively. "How do you think I know?" There was a pause while the other man spoke; then Rob laughed again. "That's right. So eat your celibate little heart out, Morton," he said.

That was when Cat decided to take his gun. Exactly what she intended to do with it, she wasn't sure; she was too hurt and angry to think straight.

She crept around the counter and moved silently up behind him. "Right," he said into the communicator. "Let me know. If I don't hear from you tonight, I'll report back in the morning."

Damn. He was hanging up. Taking the last step without regard for silence, she lunged for the gun, caught it, yanked it out of its holster, and backed away as Rob, *Agent Hepburn,* shut down the communicator, stood, and slowly turned to face her.

And she remembered what Emma had said about the danger in him. His body had gone as tense as a drawn bow. Tall and lean and midnight dark, he stood poised by the arm of the sofa, coiled aggression apparent in every bone and sinew. His eyes were fierce. They burned into her and through her, incredulous for an instant, then cynical, then hooded—fathomless pools of hidden intention. A muscle worked spasmodically in his jaw, then subsided, as if overruled by a greater power. He was hard with discipline, she realized, both physical and psychological. Tough. And about as full of human feeling and emotion as that small plastic transmitter.

What else had she expected from a man who could not love?

"Well, well," he said.

Cat replied with a crude expression that wasn't a part of her usual vocabulary and raised the gun, holding it firmly in a two-handed grip. She knew how to use it; her grandfather had taught her to handle several different types of firearms, including pistols, when she'd been a teenager. She'd never liked the things, and she'd refused to ever go out hunting with her grandfather, but she could fire it if she had to. She'd already checked the chamber and found it loaded. The safety catch was on, though; she'd made sure of that. And her aim was slightly to the left of his body.

His eyes narrowed further, if such was possible. "I don't believe it," he drawled. "I've been fooled by some women in my time, but never to this extent. Congratulations. You're one of them, I presume? So what the hell are you going to do about it—shoot me?"

"There is one particular part of you I could take great pleasure in shooting, *Agent* Hepburn," she retorted. "Then maybe it'll be you who's sitting celibate at some desk, listening to your more virile operatives crow about their conquests."

Something flashed in his eyes. "I wasn't crowing. I'm sorry you heard that. It's the way men talk."

"I've been on the road for months at a time with no one for company but men, and I know pumped-up sexual gloating when I hear it. So don't lie to me. No more lies, Hepburn, you understand me?" Her voice and hands shook. "I *hate* liars!"

Rob's cynical expression had been replaced by wariness. He took a step toward her. "Give me the gun, Cat," he said in a strangely compelling tone.

She pointedly flipped off the safety, just to convince him that she knew what she was doing. The muscle in his jaw jumped again. "Not until you answer some questions, lover-boy."

"You answer one first," he snapped. He avoided looking at the gun, but he certainly didn't act particularly intimidated. He showed no fear, no anger, no emotion at all. "Did you lure me out deliberately last night? Was something happening that I might have found out about? Had some of the contraband already arrived, for instance? Is that why you so unexpectedly capitulated after insisting there was no way you'd give your sweet body to me?"

"I don't know what you're talking about, but if you think I'm a crook, you can go straight to hell, *Agent*

Hepburn! My God, you're worse than Josh! And what did you mean when you mentioned David Kineer? Are you maniacs *still* trying to set him up? Or was it me you were going to frame this time? And for what, I'd like to know? Dealing? Possession?" She spat the words at him. "While you're at it, why not arrest me for solicitation, you foul-minded swine!"

Rob's eyes were searing into her, stripping her soul bare. After a moment, he let out a long, slow breath. "You really don't know, do you?" He muttered something extremely obscene, but there was more relief than anger in the harsh words. "Jeez, Cathy, what did you expect me to think? You sneak in here and grab my gun—of course I thought you were one of them."

"And ever since I met you, I've thought you were *not* one of them. Not a liar. Not a seducer. Not a federal drug enforcement agent or whatever the hell you are! Not another Josh!"

"I'm sorry about that, Cat." He moved almost imperceptibly toward her. "I've been sick about it, as a matter of fact."

"You're sorry! You cold-hearted bastard! I told you what Josh Evans did to me. You're even worse than he was. You *knew,* and it didn't stop you."

He advanced another step. "If you're not going to aim the gun at my body, Cat, you might as well throw the damn thing down."

Cat looked down at the gun in her hands and saw that the margin of safety in her aim had automatically increased. If it went off, it would miss him by at least three feet. If it went off. Good God, what was she trying to prove?

Rob took instant advantage of her momentary loss of eye contact. In a move so fast it made her entire world spin, he glided forward and kicked the gun out of her hands. It went flying across the room. Before it hit the floor he was on her.

Instinctively, reflexively, and with no hope of winning, Cat fought the unyielding masculine body that dragged her down. She clawed at him in fury, twisting and writhing, trying to kick him, knee him, score him with her teeth. But he was a professional. With silent, economical, and oddly *careful* force, he wrestled her to the carpet, holding her there facedown, with both arms caught behind her back.

"Let go of me!" she screamed, unable to stop the tears that had begun to fill her eyes and roll down her hot cheeks. "I wish I were living in another place, another time! I wish I weren't too civilized to shoot a hundred holes in you, Rob Hepburn!"

The pressure on her arms loosened slightly, but he continued to hold her in a grip that discouraged any further struggling. Nothing hurt, but if she continued to fight, she was afraid he might get rough. He'd never struck her as that type before, but she hadn't *known* him before, had she? She'd entrusted her body to him without feeling the slightest trace of physical fear. But now, all he would have to do was twist her arms a little, and . . .

"Relax," he said as if he'd read her mind, his breath warm and humid near her ear. "I'm not going to hurt you, Cat. I'd never hurt you." His hard thighs were straddling her bottom; she could feel the rasp of rough denim against the more fragile fabric of her light summer skirt. "You gonna settle down and listen to my explanation?"

"No! I don't want to hear it! So you'd better make the most of your superior strength and training, because the moment you let me go. I'm going to tear out your eyes!"

He chuckled, a low, sensual sound that she could actually feel up and down every muscle where his body was in contact with hers. "Little Cat. You've got claws, huh? That's okay; I don't mind that." He brought her slender wrists together so he could enclose them in one hand, then used his free hand to lift her thick hair off the back of her neck. An instant later she felt his lips there, warmly nibbling. His tongue shot out, rubbing erotically over her nape, sending shivers up and down her spine.

Oh, no, please, she begged her hormones as they treacherously started to flow. Not again. Not now. Not after what she had just learned.

"Cut it out, *Agent* Hepburn," she sneered. "Your mouth on my flesh makes me sick."

"The hell it does!"

Desperate to save herself from her own bewildering desires, she tried to strike where it would really hurt— right smack in his macho male ego. "That's right. You weren't that good, despite the sexy wall-scaler routine! I've had better, lots of times! In fact, I could teach you a few things about women and what they want, if you weren't too busy lying to people and arresting them to learn. For that matter, Josh Evans could teach you a trick or two—"

The rest of her sentence was slammed out of her as Rob flipped her onto her back. "Stop it!" he ordered, whiplash in his voice. The sight of his face, harsh and dark and stark with angry passion, shocked her. So much for his emotionless control—he was losing it now. Their gazes locked, and she stared deeply into those huge brown eyes. For an instant she seemed to be seeing clear through to the innermost chamber of his mind. And there was light there, and tenderness, and vulnerability. But then it was gone again, repressed, hidden away behind his usual mask, his usual defenses. His eyelids came down, and she stared instead at his thick dark lashes . . . the lashes she had touched gently with her lips . . . the lashes he had brushed, mothlike, against her cheeks.

"I hate you," she whispered.

"Why? Because I lied about my job? I had to lie. I had no choice."

"Because you're a liar through and through." Her voice was weary now. "Because all you are is lies."

"I'm a special agent, Ms. Holier-than-thou Mac-Farlane. I work undercover, and on no account am I allowed to go around telling people what my true profession is. That's the name of the game, lady. There are times when I don't like it; there are times, in fact, when I hate it as much as you do. But there's not one damn thing I can do about that."

She was taken aback by the roiling emotion in his words. She stared at him in silence a moment, then said, "You could quit."

"What's with you?" he shouted. "You got some grudge against the federal government? I'm here to stop a crime, to arrest a bunch of creeps. What the hell is so reprehensible about that? It's a perfectly honorable profession."

"Oh, come on, don't start waving the flag, Hepburn! I learned from Josh just how honorable you guys really are. He framed a friend of mine for a crime he didn't commit. In my book, that makes him a criminal, too."

"Maybe you just don't know the facts," he said in a hard tone.

"And maybe the facts are too *dishonorable* for you to admit! Tell me, Rob, exactly what is it that makes you different from an ordinary criminal? You carry a gun, a gun you've used to kill people with, I have no doubt. A license to kill—isn't that what they call it in the spy flicks? You thrive on adrenaline and danger—it's a high for you. Just as sex is another high. What an exciting, uncivilized life of adventure! How worthy of a Hepburn raider! Shoot the men and screw the women and hide behind the mask of a good guy, a patriot!" Once again she struggled to free herself. "You have no soul, Rob. And you really do make me sick!"

She stopped, gasping for breath, too angry—at him, at Josh, at the collapse of her futile hopes of unlocking this man and finding the heart of him—to notice the impact of her words. But she could feel the tension in his body. It was all around her—in his knees and thighs, which were pinioning her own; in his fingers, which gripped her wrists like bonds of wire; in the rock-hard sinews of his chest, which shifted ominously beneath the thin fabric of his shirt.

"You're good with words, aren't you, Catherine? A real poet in your ability to flay a man verbally. I'd match your insults against my bullets any day."

She looked up, meeting his eyes once again. The vulnerability was back, and this time he made no attempt to hide it. A pulse began to pound in her throat, and she really did feel a little ill. She had hurt him. It startled her. Nothing she had cried or cursed or shouted on the phone that final day had seemed to have much of an effect on Josh.

She tried to guard against the inevitable rush of guilt. She was soft-hearted, she knew; inflicting pain, physical or psychic, on other people had never been her thing. People who were deliberately hurtful always shocked and appalled her; it was one of the reasons she felt such instinctive distaste for any man, law enforcer or criminal, who used weapons like that gun of Rob's on their fellow human beings.

She tried to tell herself that she didn't care if he was hurt. That he had deliberately wounded her. That he had wormed his way into her bed and touched her with tenderness and passion; that he had listened to her song and made her body sing for him in a duet of such harmony, such beauty, that she had almost wept in his arms. And that it had all been nothing but a lie.

"I hate you," she repeated. "Get off me. I want to go home and take a bath. I want to wash every trace of you off my body forever."

He glared at her a moment, then smiled with his lips alone. "Liar," he said. He released her wrists and dropped his hands to her breasts, which he kneaded gently. His fingers plucked the nipples, sending spirals of fire up and down her spine. She flushed, trying with all her will to fight her body's automatic response. But as he flicked her nipples once again, a tremor passed through her. He obviously felt it, for he smiled, a tight smile reminiscent of his expression on the night when he'd so disdainfully expressed his opinion of the Project Earth Society. "You hate me, huh? You hate my touch?"

"Yes!"

One of his hands slid down to pull the blouse from her waistband so he could reach inside to caress her naked flesh. Her breasts were already swollen and aching. Her body was yearning every bit as much as her brain was protesting.

"We're going to find out about that, lady. We're going to find out exactly who tells the truth around here and who lies."

"No, damn you! No!" But her words were lost as his mouth came down on hers.

CHAPTER ELEVEN

PRESSING HER PALMS against Rob's rigid shoulders, Cat steeled herself to resist the kiss. She was determined not to give in to this very sensual man's persuasion. But before she could do much more than make her resistance obvious, Rob lifted his head. His eyes looked down into hers, a hot, direct, and deeply knowing look, a look that pinned her to the floor just as effectively as the weight of his hard-muscled body.

"Don't fight it, little liar," he said. "You're already mine. Last night took care of that."

"Last night meant *nothing*. It was just sex, just bodies."

"Liar. You gave me more than just your body last night. You gave yourself." He slid one hand into her hair and ran his thumb over her earlobe. "Your *self*, Cathy. A very sweet and generous gift, given in trust, given in love. And that's something you can never take back."

His words appalled her. Because they were true? Desperately she tried to free herself, but his knees and thighs were inexorable in their grip on her own legs. And writhing only brought her hips into closer contact with the waiting hardness in the crotch of his jeans.

"That's it," he said, grinding himself against her. "Kiss me, touch me, move with me. Show me how you really feel."

He was angry, she could tell, as angry as she. But his arousal confirmed that he was feeling the same confusing mixture of rage and desire that afflicted her. It made them partners somehow, she thought vaguely, partners in an explosive emotional confrontation neither of them had anticipated. As they had been that afternoon of the cave and the storm, they were once again at the mercy of forces they could not control. "Come on, Ms. Mac-Farlane," he added, continuing his exquisite play with her breasts, "tell me the *truth*."

"You son of a bitch!"

"Shh! No more insults, sweetheart. No more lies." He kissed her once again, then began unbuttoning her blouse and thrusting it aside. She was braless, and she shivered at the low, primal growl he made as he revealed the small firm mounds. "I'm not an agent, not here, not now," he said huskily. "I'm a man, and you, lovely lady, are a woman. My woman. That's the only truth there is between us, Cat MacFarlane. Man and woman. Lovers. Mates."

His head came down, and he gently rubbed his evening growth of whiskers against the soft flesh of her breasts, then soothed her with his oh-so-clever tongue. She moaned as sexual feeling rocketed through her, exploding in every cell, a hunger so intense she only just prevented herself from ripping at his clothes. Wretchedly, she fought against it, battling him, battling herself. Even as he pressed kisses all over her breasts, she fought him; even as his tongue flicked her nipples to agonized yearning; even as he tenderly drew her inside his hot mouth and bore down lightly with his teeth.

She whimpered, and he gave an answering growl of passion. "I love your pleasure sounds," he whispered. "That soft little moan in the back of your throat drives me crazy, sweetheart." He reared up over her and parted her legs with his knees. He slid his hands under her skirt, pushing the fabric out of his way as he caressed her thighs. One of his hands dropped to loosen his belt while the other continued to tease her, coax her, make her ready for his possession.

"Rob, please, no more. I don't want this!"

"No? I think you do." He touched her with fingers that trembled and gave her a shaky version of an ironic smile. "The truth is, your body's as eager as mine. Isn't it?" Erotically he pressed his fingers into the moist heat of her. "Admit it, Cat! You're burning for me." Lowering his body to hers, Rob sealed her mouth with his, kissing her wildly. His tongue flicked the surface of her lips, then stabbed deep into her mouth, an invasion that was almost as intimate as the hard, driving pressure against her groin.

Overwhelmed, Cat tore her mouth away from his, sucking in air and misery together. She knew she was defeated. She was burning all right; she burned everywhere he touched her. She craved the delicious slip and slide of his warm, damp flesh against her own. She wanted him to possess her, over and over, deeper and deeper, until she knew nothing but the fury of muscle against muscle, bone against bone.

He lifted his head, his handsome face predatory and hard, his brown eyes dilated to black. "The truth, Cathy," he prodded. "I want to hear you say it."

She shook her head, squeezing her eyelids against a sudden gush of tears. "Don't do this," she whispered. "Don't turn me against you; don't turn me against myself!"

But he was relentless. He drove his arousal against her, sending jolts of agonizing desire exploding through her body. "Say it, Cat!"

"All right, damn you, all right! I want you. I need you so much it hurts." She opened her eyes and looked directly into his. "There, Hepburn. You win. Are you happy now? Does it make you feel virile and potent and proud to know you've so thoroughly defeated me?"

His gaze didn't waver. They stared into each other's minds and hearts and souls in an exchange so intimate it left her reeling. Then, slowly, his triumph faded, to be replaced by something so bleak, so miserable, so full of agony that Cat felt her heart clutch and falter in her breast. Instinctively her hands tightened on his shoulders. *It's all right,* she wanted to whisper. *Don't look like that, please!*

"No," he muttered. "It makes me feel like the son of a bitch you assured me I was." Then he pushed himself up and off her, rolling over smoothly and springing to his feet with hard, athletic grace.

Shivering with reaction, Cat turned over on her side and brought her legs up to her chest. Her tears flowed freely; she made no attempt to stop them. Rob watched her for a moment, his guts twisting with despair. He was sweating; he was shaking. And his own eyes, he realized vaguely, were stinging with unshed—unsheddable—tears.

Feelings were ricocheting through him, emotions he hadn't felt for years. Anger, guilt, and a towering sexual tension that made him want to rip the clothes from her body and drive himself so deeply into her that he would lose his identity in hers. And it would be well lost, he told himself bitterly. For he didn't like the self she had forced him to reveal.

A man without love. A man without a soul. Was that the truth, *his* truth? A wave of nausea took him. What if she was right?

For a long time there was silence in the room. Rob had stalked to the window; he stared out into darkness, hearing the sound of the waves pounding the cliffs. Darkness, his darkness. The place where he was lost. The glass provided a slight reflection; in it he could see the brightness of Cat's hair spread out wildly on the floor, its red highlights shimmering in the light from the kitchenette. Sun-child, born of light. Her light was strong enough to show his darkness for what it was. He swallowed, once again feeling the almost intolerable pressure of his tears. He hadn't cried since Beth had died. He'd sworn then that he would never cry again.

When the silence in the room grew oppressive, Cat slowly sat up. With trembling fingers she rebuttoned her blouse after drying her cheeks with its hem. She pulled down her skirt. She scooted back against the sofa and leaned her head against a cushion. She couldn't get up; her legs weren't ready to hold her weight.

Hearing her move, Rob turned to face her. "I'm sorry," he said, his words clipped and short. "That was unforgivable, inexcusable. It was domination of the vilest and most despicable kind. It proves nothing, reveals no truth except the fact of my own selfishness and pride. Everything you said about me was right."

Cat stared quizzically at him, his tall, lean body standing there so beautiful and straight. *He looks so sad. How utterly alone he is.*

"You hate me, and I don't blame you," he went on. "I hate myself."

"Oh, Rob—"

"Please go. I can't trust myself; you make me crazy. I've never done anything like that before, and I still want you enough to throw you down and . . . Please, just go."

She drew a deep breath. "There's something I'd like to say to you first."

When he didn't look at her or react, she continued. "When we met, I knew it would be a mistake to get mixed up with you. Oh, I wanted you—that was true from the moment I looked up from my singing and met your eyes across the room. And I felt you stake your claim on me; I knew that I would run and you would follow, just as I knew you would eventually hunt me down."

He grimaced but did not interrupt.

"When I decided to sleep with you, I knew it was a foolish thing to do. I saw the pain waiting for me; I already felt the heartache. But I did it anyway. Do you want to know why?"

He had closed his eyes. "Tell me why."

"For the silliest—and the most feminine—reason in the world. I hoped I could change you. I hoped that by sharing my music, my illusions with you, I would find and touch your heart." She stopped, her bottom lip quivering.

"You're very generous," he said softly. "But there's no heart in me to find."

"Not generous!" she snapped, her tone derisive now. Self-derisive. "I wasn't doing it out of kindness. I wanted something in return! I'm lonely, too, Hepburn! My songs don't keep me warm and comforted in the deepest cold of nigh' She bit her lip, adding, "I wanted you to love me. Isn't that what everybody wants?"

"I don't know." He sounded miserable.

"I knew it wasn't possible, but deep down I must have had some hope. I can't imagine why. It's just that there was something about you, something I felt or sensed or—oh, God! I should have known it last night, when, as always, you got me to talk but wouldn't tell me anything about yourself, anything substantial, anything real. You didn't want me to get to know you; you didn't share the little confidences all lovers share."

"I couldn't tell you anything. You understand why now."

"No, Rob—that's an excuse. You couldn't tell me

what you were here on this island for, but you had a life,
I presume, before you took up your profession. You even
had a wife. Or was that another lie?"

When he avoided her eyes instead of answering, she
groaned, saying, "Don't tell me that was the finishing
touch to your seduction? I was filled with compassion
for you because of your supposedly dead wife and the
bitterness that loss must have left in you. But if that,
too, was a lie..."

"Cat." He came back across the room and knelt on
the floor at her feet. He didn't touch her, but she could
feel the heat his body radiated. "That wasn't a lie. All I
lied to you about was the reason for my presence on this
island. I didn't tell you about Beth and how she died
because it's not something I care to remember. I've never
discussed her death with anyone."

"Never? In eight years you've never been close enough
to *anyone* to discuss the subject?"

He stared into her green eyes, hearing her incredulity.
It was true: In eight years there had been no one he'd
entrusted with the story of Beth's death. No one he'd
felt close enough to. "She was murdered," he said. "By
terrorists. In front of my eyes. And there wasn't a thing
I could do to save her." He ignored Cat's gasp and went
on. "Her father worked for the State Department. So did
mine. But her dad was top brass and controversial, and
Beth was his only relative, the only person he had. The
only person *I* had."

"Dear God." Cat took a breath and blew it out. "You
don't have to tell me."

"I want to," he said, shaking his head a little because
he *did* want to. "We were traveling in Europe one summer
vacation—both of us were graduate students during the
school year. We'd been married not quite a year. We
were in Paris, staying with her dad. Although we'd been
provided with security, we were young and cocky and

didn't think it was necessary. We slipped the guard one evening and went out for a romantic evening on the town. That was when they got us. Both of us. I wasn't important, though. Beth was the real hostage. They wanted to get to her dad through her."

Cat murmured something—he wasn't sure what—and took his hands in hers. "At the time it happened you wouldn't have caught me waving any patriotic flags. I'd been dragged all over the world with my diplomat parents, and for the most part, I'd hated it. My mother was dead, and my father was drinking too much. I had no other close relatives. Beth was the center of my world.

"But nothing I'd ever experienced prepared me for the terrorists. They were young and cruel and absolutely certain their cause was just. Amateurs, really. Fanatics. You couldn't argue with them—it was as if they'd been brainwashed. They had a long list of ridiculous demands, including money, the release of several of their imprisoned friends, and the surrender of Beth's father, whom they intended to try for crimes against the proletariat or some such thing. They were arrogant and utterly unrealistic. They couldn't believe it when they were told their demands would not be met." He paused a moment. "That was when they decided to get rough with us. They wanted the authorities to know they meant business."

"Rob, please, you needn't relive this for my sake." Cat was kneeling beside him now, practically in his lap. "I don't want you to suffer through it all again just because I complained that I didn't know anything about you."

"It's all right. Maybe I need to talk about it, after all. And I do want you to know, Cathy. Maybe you'll understand me better if you know."

Cat heard the wistful note in his voice. It clutched at her emotions, and she knew in that moment that she was going to forgive him for everything—his lies, his profession, his attempt to manipulate her with sex. She cursed herself for a soft-hearted idiot, but what could she do? It was not in her nature to hold on to her anger for long.

"I won't inflict all the details upon you; suffice it to say that we were tortured, both mentally and physically. Beth, too—they didn't treat her any more gently than they treated me." He spoke very coldly now, as if control were imperative. "She was defiant and brave—too defiant for her own good. At one point she was struggling with them, and somebody hit her. She fell back against a concrete bulkhead in the cellar where they were keeping us and cracked her head." He shuddered. "She was dazed afterward—she probably had a concussion. She flipped out and started screaming, unnerving the terrorists. One of them raised his gun, but she paid no attention to him. He told her to stop it, but she didn't. There was an explosion. I still hear it sometimes, in my dreams. I don't think he really meant to kill her. I think he just wanted to shut her up."

"Oh, my God!"

"The worst was, I couldn't do anything. *Anything*. I would have stopped her screaming if they'd let me hold her, talk to her, soothe her. But I was tied up and gagged. I had to watch the entire horror being acted out in front of me while I lay there, completely helpless. I couldn't even hold her afterward, while she was still warm, while she still looked like my wife. I couldn't cry over her; I couldn't mourn. The government commandos attacked as soon as they heard the shots, and by time I was released from the hospital—I was pretty seriously injured during the raid—Beth had long been lying in her grave."

Cat was crying. For Beth, who'd died so violently; for Rob, who'd had to live with such terrible memories. Silent tears were sliding one after another down her cheeks. He touched them, gently, with the tip of one finger, then put the finger to his lips.

"I had never felt so powerless. I swore I would never be powerless again. You've seen the results. I went home, quit grad school, quit my job as a part-time astronomer, and learned to shoot a gun. I asked my father to pull some strings so I could get an Agency job. They almost didn't take me. They said I was too emotional, if you can believe that." He laughed harshly. "But I was smart and tough and physically fit, not to mention a whiz at languages, so, after some hesitation, they reconsidered and signed me up. And I proved to be clever at sublimating my emotions. Very clever indeed." He cupped his hands under her chin and raised her tear-stained face to his. "Far too clever, it seems."

Cat blinked at him and tried to smile. She was reeling inside. So much had happened in the last hour that she was having a hard time keeping up with it all. Rob Hepburn had gone from being an astronomer to an undercover agent . . . her lover to a stranger . . . a man she was falling in love with to a man she had wanted very much to despise.

And yet he'd just shared something with her that he'd never told anybody else, something that made her cry for him, pity him, ache to comfort him. He'd given her a piece of himself, a very deep and private piece, and how she responded, she sensed, was very important. He was waiting. His eyes were dark with an enigmatic expression in which she thought she could read sadness mingled with—what? Hope? Or fear? What did he want from her? What was she still willing to give?

Your self. A very sweet and generous gift, given in trust, given in love.

Dear God. It was true: She *was* going to forgive him. What he had told her had only confirmed what she had guessed from the start—that there were hidden depths to this man that were worth plumbing no matter what obstacles remained in the way. Did it really matter what he did for a living? She loved him. Whatever he could or couldn't offer her, she loved him anyway. She was already committed, as she had known she would be from the moment she had given her body into his keeping.

"Rob?"

"What?"

"Do you want the truth? The real truth?"

His expression changed—tightened. He dropped his hands into his lap and looked defeated. "I think maybe I've had enough truths for one night."

"Well, here's one more anyway. I sang to you last night because I'd fallen in love with you." She smiled. "Will you let me sing to you again tonight?"

He stared, pale and wretched. "No, sweetheart," he whispered. "Not again. Not because you feel sorry for me."

"I don't feel—"

"Cat. I've just told you a sad story, but I didn't tell it in an eleventh-hour bid to win your sympathy and approval. You hate me, remember? I'm the swine who lied to you and seduced you."

She took one of his hands and placed it on her breast. He gasped, tearing it away as if she'd burned him. She smiled, then actually laughed. "What, shy, Hepburn? Is this the same man who scaled a castle wall to reach my bedroom last night?"

His eyes took on dangerous glints of color. "I'm trying to be noble, dammit, Cat! I'm trying to keep my gun-toting hands off your tempting little body. But don't press your luck!"

She rose from the floor and bent over to inspect the sofa bed. "This thing opens up, I presume? I'm stiff from our romantic interlude in the pine needles, and I'd prefer to make love on a mattress tonight, if you don't mind."

"Cat!"

She tossed the pillows to the floor and jerked the mattress out. The mechanism squeaked and protested, and the mattress, when it appeared, looked old and thin and lumpy. She sighed philosophically, then began un-buttoning her blouse.

Rob swallowed hard, his dilated pupils following her every move. "I'll give you till the count of three to get the hell out of here, woman. If you don't leave, I won't be responsible for my actions. One . . ."

She tossed off the blouse and reached around her back for the zipper on her skirt. Moments later the light fabric was falling around her ankles. She stepped out of it and slid her fingers inside the elastic waistband of her panties.

"Two . . ." said Rob hoarsely.

"Please don't stare like a wild beast contemplating its supper." She smiled as she slid the panties down. "I've never been particularly proud of my body, and you're embarrassing me."

"You have a beautiful body," he murmured. "All slen-der curves and supple muscles. You have no idea how much your body excites me, Cathy. I just have to look at you, and I—"

"I know," she whispered. "Your body does something similar to me." She sat down on the mattress and slid under the sheet.

"Three."

"I'm still here."

"So I see."

"You've still got your clothes on. Why don't you take them off, turn out the light, and come to bed?"

"Cat, you're going to regret this."

"Maybe. Maybe not."

"I'm no good for you, Cat."

"No? Listen:

> "There once was good-looking spy
> Who appeared to be sexually shy,
> But when coaxed into bed,
> His modesty fled,
> And he proved most deliciously spry!"

There was dead silence for an instant; then Rob laughed softly, and she knew everything was going to be all right. He shucked his shirt, stepped out of his jeans, and flipped off the light, casting the room into total darkness. Then Cat felt the mattress sink and shift under his weight. As she turned to him, he opened his arms for her and seemed to envelop her completely. His hands pressed her flat, one thigh covered hers, and his hard chest came down upon her small soft breasts. She could feel his arousal against the side of her hip.

His breath fanned her lips, but the awaited kiss didn't come. Instead he whispered,

> "There once was a hard-*headed* dame,
>   Who left all her lovers aflame
>   Till along came a Scot
>   So demanding and hot
>   That she opened her legs and made sweet
>   love to him all night long."

"That doesn't rhyme! Or scan!"

"But it's bawdy," he countered. "Anyway, I never claimed to be a poet, did I?"

"Oh, Rob..."

"Do it."

"Do what?"

"Make my limerick come true."

"Uh...there."

"Good God, Cathy—"

"Love me, Rob."

He loved her into boneless, mindless, soul-shattering oblivion.

CHAPTER TWELVE

ROB AND CAT were interrupted about an hour later by the buzzing of Rob's telecommunicator. Groaning, he rolled over and reached for it, giving her a rueful look as he spoke into the phone. "Yeah," he growled, then swore. "Okay. Right." He sat up, pushed the sheet out of the way, and grabbed his jeans. "I'm on it, Morton, so stop worrying," he finished, and broke the connection.

"What is it?" she asked as he rose and stepped into his pants.

"It seems our clever boys at the other end missed the fact that one of the boats had already moved out, headed for Aberdeen Island, yesterday. The other is on its way now, too. Some of the guns, in other words, are already here."

His cover blown anyway, Rob had given her the details of the case after they'd made love. Cat's protests that Dave Kineer couldn't possibly be involved in anything so sordid had persisted even as he'd told her the facts. She was troubled and confused, but Rob seemed to be so sure . . . as Josh had apparently been last year. She thought back on some of the things Josh had said to her and was suddenly able to see them in a new light. It wasn't drugs that Josh had suspected her of being mixed up with. It was *weapons,* for godsake. High-powered rifles, mortars, and explosives manufactured in the U.S., purchased illegally or stolen, and sold to foreign intermediaries for use by criminals, insurgents, and terrorists abroad.

Terrorists like the ones who had murdered Rob's wife.

"What are you going to do?" she asked.

He shrugged into his shirt and buckled on his shoulder holster. The gun itself he retrieved from the floor on the far side of the room. "I've got to try to get a fix on them," he said. "So far I've been unable to figure out where they're going to bring in their boats and stash the contraband, so the best I can do is hang around the airstrip, in case they try to carry out the transfer operation tonight. It's unlikely, with the cloud cover, but if they went ahead and I wasn't there, my whole assignment would have been an expensive, wasted effort." He looked at her thoughtfully. "You know this island, Cat. If you were a smuggler, where would you bring in your boat?"

"Well, the western side of the island is where the beaches are—not that anybody ever goes swimming, but people do sunbathe. There are too many houses and vacation homes . . . too risky. But the currents are tricky on the eastern side, and the coastline is rocky and wild. Very treacherous, and there's no good place to land a boat."

"That's the impression I got. Which leaves . . ."

"The southern tip, where the town and the harbor are. Too public—we can rule that out, can't we? That eliminates everywhere except the north, where the lobstermen fish. But they're often out at night or in the early morning, so the north isn't a very private or secure area, either."

"I've had this identical discussion with myself a dozen times," he said in disgust. "For some reason I keep having the niggling feeling that I'm missing something."

"What do you mean? Like what?"

"I feel as if I ought to know where these creeps are landing, but for some reason I don't." He shrugged impatiently. "Never mind. I'm pretty sure about the airstrip, at least. I can stake that out, and—"

"Rob, wait. Pirates' Cove—have you considered Pirates' Cove? It's on the uninhabited eastern side of the island, and while it certainly isn't much of a landing site, it *is* marginally possible to bring a boat in there, particularly if the boat is small."

"The place where we had our picnic?"

"Yes!" She was excited now. "They could be hiding their weapons in the cave."

Rob swore. He clapped the heel of his hand against his forehead, muttering, "You're slipping, man, slipping. Why the *hell* didn't I think of that myself? A large cave in a private cove within hiking distance of the airstrip. Of course!"

"You think that's it?"

"Yes, dammit, I think that's it. And if I hadn't been keeping that spot in my mind as a place of pleasant, sexy memories, I'd have realized it long before this!"

They exchanged a hot-eyed look.

"But the cave is well hidden. Hardly anybody except a few islanders know it's there. Lovers use it occasionally, and children playing—"

"Were you ever there with a lover?" he demanded.

"I? No, I—"

"Were you there with Evans?" he snapped, astonished by the anger that ripped through him at the thought.

"No. I was never there with a lover before you. I did

take some friends there once, when a similar squall came up."

"The members of your band." It was not a question.

"Yes," she whispered. "David Kineer was one of them."

He looked at her but didn't say *I told you so*. Cat swallowed hard. There must be some mistake. Not David. The whole band had been there that day; it must have been somebody else. She refused to believe that David, whom she had always liked and trusted, could be a criminal.

"Are you going over there?" she asked Rob dully.

"Yes. If our theory is correct, they'll be there—some of them—at the cave tonight."

"But what if they see you? What if you get caught?"

"They're not going to see me. I'll be checking it out tonight, that's all. We'll wait to nail them when they transfer the guns to the plane."

"How many smugglers are there?"

"Four, plus the pilot. But one of them's really one of ours, working undercover."

"That's still three against two."

"For now, yes. The Agency's sending in a backup for the bust tomorrow." He returned to the sofa bed and stroked his hand through her hair. "Worried about me, love? I've been doing this kind of work for a long time, you know."

"What if something goes wrong?" she asked uneasily.

"Nothing's going to go wrong." He reached down and scooped up her blouse and skirt. "Come on. Up, pretty lady. I'll see you back to the castle to make sure you're safely home."

Silently Cat accepted her clothes and began to dress. Rob had turned cold and businesslike again. The tough, hard-eyed pro. Mr. Unreachable. Their lovemaking had been beautiful, more tender and fulfilling than ever before. He had laughed with her and talked for the first time, revealing more about his lonely, rootless childhood, his parents, Beth. He'd given her hope that maybe, just *maybe,* there was a chance for this relationship, after all.

But now . . . "Rob?" she said as they finished dressing and moved toward the door.

"Yeah, sun-child?"

"If you bust these guys tomorrow night and everything does go according to plan, your work here will be finished, won't it?"

He stared down at her, his dark eyes unreadable in the dim light. There was a pause of several heartbeats before he sighed and said, "Yes."

She waited, but he added nothing more.

Head bowed, she walked quietly out to her car with Rob following a pace behind.

It was just after ten when they got back to the castle. Rob got out of the car and explained he would go by foot across to the old runway, then on over to the coastal highway and the cove.

"As for you, tonight you stay in the castle," he ordered as he pulled her close for a deeply passionate kiss. "No wandering out in the woods, singing. There are criminals around. I want you safe."

"Are you kidding? I have no desire to tangle with a bunch of desperadoes, I assure you!"

"I'll call you in the morning."

"Be careful, Rob," she whispered, clinging just a little.

He kissed her one more time and let her go, giving her a confident wave as he descended the slope behind the castle in the direction of the airstrip.

Morosely Cat went inside. She couldn't help being afraid for him, although she told herself over and over that he was an expert at this and knew exactly what he was doing. The fact that she would have preferred him to be an expert at almost any other line of work was something she tried to put out of her mind.

"Where's Granddad?" she inquired of Mrs. Baldwin, who was sitting in front of the TV, watching the latest installment of her favorite prime time soap opera. Cat was surprised not to find her grandfather waiting for her, suspiciously demanding where the devil she had been all evening.

"You just missed him. He went out with that fisher-man—what's his name, Jon Hayden. Said they were going out to watch for the spaceship Jon claims to have seen last night. Not that I hold with this flying saucer business," Mrs. Baldwin added with a snort of contempt. "Bunch of silliness, if you ask me."

"Oh, dear, I wish he wouldn't do this sort of thing! He's getting too old to be chasing around the island at night."

Mrs. Baldwin grunted her agreement.

"Did they say exactly where they were going?" Cat asked.

"Over to Pirates' Cove, I imagine. Same place he saw the thing last night," said Mrs. Baldwin disinterestedly.

Cat swayed slightly and had to clutch the nearest chair-back. "Pirates' Cove? Is that where Jon saw the lights last night?"

"That's what they told me," Mrs. Baldwin confirmed.

Dear God. Sweat broke out on Cat's palms. Even now her grandfather and young Jon Hayden might be blithely walking into a den of thieves! "How long ago did they leave?"

"'Bout ten minutes ago, no more. Took Jon's pickup truck. Went 'round by the coast road, I imagine, although if they'd listened to my opinion—Cat, where're you off to, girl?"

"I've got to stop them!" Cat shouted as she ran out of the room.

Cat called for Rob in the garden behind the castle,

but he had disappeared. She let loose with a full range
of expletives that she'd forgotten she knew. Regretfully
she realized she would have to disobey his orders about
staying safe in the castle tonight. Granddad was in danger. She raced back to the driveway, jumped into her car,
started it, swung it around, and put her foot to the floor.
She had to try to reach her grandfather and Jon before
they got to Pirates' Cove . . . before they found themselves in a jam not even the benevolent aliens from the
Project Earth Society could extricate them from.

Cat was within half a mile of the cove on the treacherously curving coastal road when she grimly conceded
that she wasn't going to overtake her grandfather. He
and Jon had obviously had too much of a start on her.
They were already there, dammit; they might already be
in the hands of the smugglers. "Damn, damn, damn!"
she whispered, forcing herself to slow the car and approach the site more carefully. The rocky path that led
down to the cove was around that next sharp curve in
the road. Maybe she'd better leave her car here, where
it wouldn't be seen.

Parking well off to the side of the road, Cat trudged
the rest of the way on foot. She moved as silently as
possible, keeping her eyes on the rocks and bushes she
passed for any sign of Rob. Somewhere he, too, was
sneaking up on the smugglers. But he wouldn't be here
yet, she reminded herself. Even though he'd taken a more
direct route, she'd still have gotten here faster by car
than he could have on foot.

At least when he did arrive, he would know what to
do. For the first time she felt thankful for Rob's professional abilities.

Ten feet from the pathway that led to Pirates' Cove,
Cat found Jon Hayden's pickup truck parked. It was
empty, and there was no sign of either man. Oh, hell!

She peered into the front and saw her grandfather's tam-o'-shanter lying on the passenger's seat. Grimacing, she looked down the hill toward the sea. He was out there somewhere, a balmy old Scot of his advanced age, climbing down a rough, rocky path in search of a phantom UFO! Under her breath, Cat muttered, "Oh, you silly, silly man!"

Plunging her fists into the pockets of her Irish knit sweater, Cat went around the pickup and stealthily set foot upon the path that led down to the sea. It was foggy and stormy out. In the distance she could hear thunder growling. Down below, the rough waves crashed against the rocks. And then she heard something else: a shout, a loud highlands curse, and the muffled but unmistakable report of a gun.

No! Gasping with fear for her grandfather—the one man who'd always been there for her, the one man whose love she'd never doubted for so much as a moment—Cat began to run down the path toward the sound. She'd gone about twenty yards when, out of the darkness, a shadow hurled itself at her and flung her to the ground. She fell facedown, the wind knocked out of her by the impact. She whimpered, conscious of scraped knees, a bump on her chin, and the sharp pain caused by the way her assailant was dragging her wrists up behind her back. Oh, idiot, idiot! Rob hadn't hurt her like this when he'd held her down.

She winced and struggled uselessly as rough hands turned her over and pulled her up to an unsteady kneeling position. She opened her eyes . . . and looked into the all-too-familiar face of David Kineer.

"Sorry, luv," he said in the fake British accent he had been affecting for years. "I know you like this spot, but believe me, this was one night you and your crazy grand-daddy shouldn't have chosen to chase after UFO's."

"David? Oh, David, not you!"

"My sentiments exactly. I always liked you, luv, innocent and credulous though you were. Why the hell couldn't you have stayed home tonight?" He jerked her roughly to her feet. "Come on, let's go."

Cat stumbled as she felt the nose of a handgun jab the small of her back. "What are you doing, David? Are you crazy? And where's my grandfather? If you've hurt him..."

"He and his friend are in the cave. Nobody's been hurt so far, but..." His voice trailed off ominously. He had released her wrists, but his hands were heavy on her shoulders as he hustled her down the path. Cat's fingers automatically went to her grandmother's necklace, worrying it nervously.

"My, er, associates are not pleased with this development," David went on. "If it were just me, I wouldn't touch you, but they'll probably insist on silencing that lovely voice of yours. You shouldn't have poked your nose where you don't belong. You're about to sing your swan song, I'm afraid. Now move."

"David, you and I have been friends for a long time. Surely you wouldn't turn me over to your—your associates, and—"

"Shut up, Cat! It's your own damn fault! Anyway, you're no friend of mine. I didn't see you rushing to my aid last year when I got arrested by that son of a bitch secret agent."

"Who was right about you, after all!" she retorted. "They should have locked you up and thrown away the key!"

"Just move, baby," he said, giving her a shove that almost toppled her again. Cat tugged so hard on her gold locket that the catch released and the chain came loose in her hand. It slipped through her numb fingers and vanished onto the rocky path beneath their feet.

Cat moaned softly at the loss of her protective talisman. Choking back a sob, she made no further protest as her former friend David marched her down the rocky path to Pirates' Cove.

CHAPTER THIRTEEN

WHEN ROB HEPBURN glided shadowlike down the hill to the coast road a few hundred feet before the path that led to Pirates' Cove and discovered Cat's car parked on the side of the road, he was hit with an almost paralyzing blow of disbelief. His first thought was that she'd come tearing over here out of some misguided need to help or watch over him. His second, far more demoralizing thought was that she might be in with the smugglers after all. She might have hurried here to warn her old friend David. Perhaps she'd been in touch with him all along.

No, he insisted. *No.* Not Cat. He'd been wrong about women before, yeah, but this woman he'd held close to his heart, loved, tasted—God, the taste of her flesh was on his lips even now. He'd let her get to him; he'd opened up his heart to her. For the first time in years he'd let his defenses down. He'd trusted her, been sure of her, believed in her music, her poetry, her songs.

He'd even begun to believe in her love.

These thoughts flashed through Rob's stunned brain as he stood there, one arm resting on the roof of Cat's car. He'd begun to feel tonight that he might be able to love again, after all. Had it all been a trick, an *illusion?*

Think, Hepburn. No, don't think. Don't use your brain, your reason. Try using your heart.

Put that way, it was easy. His heavy spiritedness slipped away, and for several moments he was furiously angry with himself instead. What the hell was he doing, suspecting Cathy now? Had his years in the Agency really made him so cynical, so mistrustful, so hard? She loved him, God help her. She loved him a helluva lot more than he deserved.

God, maybe he'd better get out of this racket. Abruptly he remembered something a senior agent had once told him—Francis O'Brien, the man who had trained him: *You know you're used up when you start doubting your judgments, your actions, your gut responses. You ever feel like that, you know it's time to quit.*

Taking his own advice, O'Brien had quit the Agency not long after making that statement. Rob had heard he was married now and the proud father of a baby girl.

"Lucky man," Rob muttered.

He forced his mind back to the job at hand, but he was feeling shaky, and—why not admit it?—frightened by the presence of Cat's car. His gun held ready in his hand, he silently advanced along the road. Around the next curve, he found the pickup truck with Duncan MacFarlane's cap inside. He recognized the truck—Jon Hayden had been sitting on it, drinking a bottle of beer, the day Rob had interviewed him about his UFO sighting.

He swore. The situation was suddenly clear. Cat's grandfather had come chasing UFO's with Hayden, and Cat, knowing the danger, had come chasing Granddad. More rapidly now, his blood pounding with a fierce upsurge of adrenaline, Rob moved onto the path that would

lead him to the cove where he had first tried to make
love to Cat. His senses were extra-alert, watching for
any sign of a lookout, any sign of a threat—which was
probably what enabled him to pick out the dim glow of
gold beneath his feet. He stooped and recovered the delicate necklace Cat wore night and day around her throat.
*I wear it as a good luck charm. My grandmother once
told me it would protect me in times of danger. I know
it's crazy and superstitious, but, still, I never take it off.*
    Rob took the remainder of the slope at a dead run.

Inside the cave where David dragged her, Cat was
confronted with three tough-looking smugglers, a load
of wooden crates and boxes, and, huddled in one corner
under a hanging oil lantern, her grandfather and Jon
Hayden, securely bound with rope. Neither of them appeared to be wounded, she saw with great relief. The
shot she had heard had apparently gone wide.
    Her arrival caused an outbreak of cursing and swearing
among the smugglers, and a heated argument over what
was to be done with her and their other hapless prisoners.
One man favored killing them all immediately. The second, looking her over with an undisguised leer, suggested
killing the two men and reserving her for a different fate.
The third, a kinky-haired man with stark, almost-too-
perfect features and a thick beard, said nothing, but he
stared at her in a manner that for some reason made her
more nervous than anything else he could have said or
done.
    One of these men, Cat reminded herself, was, like
Rob, a federal agent. She sneaked glances at them all.
Which one? They all looked murderously sinister to her.
    David pushed her roughly over to the corner where
the other prisoners were. She could see her grandfather's
despairing eyes; he would have yelled at her, she was
sure, if his mouth had not been gagged. Cat winced under

his stare and touched his shoulder gently in the moment before the bearded man came up behind her, took her wrists, and efficiently tied her arms behind her back. She ignored him. "Don't worry," she said bracingly to Grand-dad. "We'll get out of this, I promise."

The smuggler turned her around to face him. "Sit down, lady, and close your mouth," he said. "One more sound and I'll do something to you that'll shut those pretty green eyes for a long, long time."

Cat felt a shiver along her spine, but it wasn't from fear. Confused, she stared at her captor. Surely she knew that voice—she'd heard it in the dark so many countless times. But it couldn't be. It wasn't. For a moment those eyes met hers, and they were a vivid blue, not the slate gray that Josh's eyes had been. The nose was different, and the cheekbones, even the lips. Josh's hair had been a shade or two lighter, and straight as parallel lines. This man's hair was a midnight-black mass of curls.

Was there a flash of something in those unfamiliar eyes? Reassurance? Forbearance? What?

"Down," he repeated.

He didn't sound like Josh, she decided this time. His voice had an odd nasal quality she didn't recognize at all.

Shaken, she sat down as ordered. She discovered that her wrists had not been tightly bound. If she worked them a bit, she suspected she could free them.

It wasn't Josh—of course it wasn't Josh. But the bearded man, she was almost sure of it, was Rob's fellow federal agent.

Leaning her head against her grandfather's shoulder, Cat listened intently to the low and sometimes angry voices of the gunrunners. Oh, Rob, she was thinking, I'm so sorry. He no longer had a simple smuggling operation on his hands. He had hostages to contend with. One of whom was his lover.

She tried not to think about what had happened to his wife. She prayed he wouldn't think about it, although she knew he would. You're not helpless anymore, she told him mentally. And besides, I promise you, I'm not going to let them kill me.

"They ought to have been here by now," David Kineer was complaining, his voice high pitched and nervous. He kept going to the mouth of the cave and looking out to sea. "If they don't get here soon, the fog'll come in solid and they'll crack up on the damn rocks."

"The seas are rough," the bearded one said. "The going's slow. They'll be here."

"They'd better be. We need those two to help shift this stuff to the airstrip. It's several hours work as it is, and if we expect to get it done before dawn, when the pilot's flying in, we need to get to work!"

"Cool it, Kineer," one of the others said. "We got time."

Uh-oh, Cat was thinking. When the other boat arrived, there would be five bad guys, not three. Six, with the pilot of the plane. The plane that was flying in tonight, not tomorrow night. Rob's information, she realized with a shudder, was inaccurate.

Was he out there? she wondered. He must be; he'd said he would be. Had he seen her car? He must have seen Jon's pickup truck; he must have formed some conclusions as to what was going on. He might even be scouting around the cave at this very moment.

But what could he do? Here in the cave, with three hostages and hundreds of pounds of weapons, the criminals were untouchable. Rob *was* helpless. Even if he'd had ten men to back him up, he wouldn't have been able to do a thing. If only she could get some of the smugglers out of the cave. If only she could get *herself* out of the cave. And quickly, before the second boat arrived to complicate matters further.

The second boat . . . "Uh, excuse me," she said.

Four malevolent pairs of eyes shifted in her direction. Cat shivered. You'd better make this good, she ordered herself.

"I thought I told you, lady, to shut up?" the bearded man said. But he made no move toward her.

"Yes, I know you did, but I couldn't help over-hearing," she said apologetically. "I think I may have some information about your friends. The ones on the boat you're looking for? I think I may know why they haven't arrived."

"What the hell do you mean?" cried David.

"You didn't give me a chance to explain what I was doing here, David. I certainly wasn't searching for UFO's! I came looking for my grandfather and Jon, to get their help. You see, I was driving home from a visit to a friend when I spotted a wreck on the rocks about half a mile from here—a small boat of some kind—a real mess, with crates and boxes spilled out all over the place. I couldn't see any sign of survivors, but it was dark and I had no equipment and I knew my grandfather was here somewhere, searching for flying saucers . . ."

She had gotten no more than halfway through this speech when the cursing started. Suddenly four men were surrounding her, shooting questions at her that she tried her best to answer without inconsistency. Had she notified the authorities? No, there wasn't time. Had anyone else seen the wreck? No, she was alone, and it had obviously just happened. These crates and boxes—were they broken open? Could she see what was inside? No, she hadn't cared about cargo, dammit; she'd been worrying about the people. She was the only one with that concern, it seemed. One of the crooks was moaning and groaning about the loss of his precious guns, while David was muttering anxiously about the possibility of getting caught by the Coast Guard or the FBI.

The bearded man, who seemed to have appointed himself the leader in this moment of crisis, reached down and hauled Cat to her feet. She came eagerly, faintly cheered that her spur-of-the-moment plan was working so well. "Come on," he said gruffly. "You come with me, Kineer, and you, too, Baylor. Amato, you stay here and watch over these bozos." He waved a hand with a gun in it at Duncan MacFarlane and Jon Hayden. "As for you," he said to Cat, "you're gonna show us where you spotted this wreck. And you'd better be tellin' the truth, or I'm personally gonna drill you, baby, and toss your body into the sea."

Great, thought Cat. If the man was acting, he was doing a convincing job of it. And if he wasn't . . . she was very much afraid she wouldn't live to see the dawn.

When the first man started out of the cave, Rob's hope and anticipation soared. He quickly ducked out of sight behind an outcrop of rock, readying his gun and wishing he had a high-powered rifle. He also wished the fog were not so soup-thick. It had been getting worse every minute—the fog and the wind and the wild spewing of the cold waves. A squall, he suspected, was about to hit the island.

He'd ascertained, to his dismay, that Cat, her grandfather, and Jon Hayden were indeed prisoners. There were four men guarding them, he'd discovered during his own brief and risky glance into the cavern, gleaned from a prone position with his legs knee-deep in icy water. He'd moved off, then, trying to decide what in hell to do.

The first few moments after that glimpse of the interior of the cave had been pretty rocky. He'd crouched there, wet and uncaring, trapped in a private nightmare, a deep black tunnel of déjà vu.

It was Beth all over again. The guns, the desperadoes,

the hostages, the night. A woman, *his* woman, trapped in the hands of evil men who had no care for human life, who would kill without a qualm. Over the years he'd met many such, but not since that first tragic experience with Beth had he ever had anything emotional at stake. No one he loved had been threatened; not until now, not until tonight.

Gone was Rob's conviction about his inability to love. He'd been a fool—oh, God, such a fool! He loved Cat MacFarlane; he knew it now. He loved her warmth and her humor, the piercing beauty of her songs, the quick wit of her limericks. He loved her courage and opti-mism—the two qualities that had persuaded her to take a chance on him, even though she had been hurt before. He loved her sweet, sweet body, her hair like spun fire, her deep green Siren eyes.

He loved her, and he was terrified that he was going to lose her to a bullet in the dark.

Just like Beth.

Slowly, very slowly, he had calmed himself. It was almost as if *she* were calming him. He imagined her telling him that it was all right, that it was different this time, that she was determined not to die. He tried very hard to believe it.

Slowly, because he loved her, he ordered himself to put all fear completely out of his mind. He had to act as he had been trained to do, skillfully, mechanically, with total concentration and control. He had to forget every-thing that was at stake here and pretend it was just another job. There was nothing else to do. If he gave in to the terror that was coursing inside him, he would freeze and be unable to act. Then somebody *would* die.

Inside that cave, he knew, there was one man who would support him. He didn't know his name or his cover, but he had his description. Tall, bearded, with a head of kinky hair. Two agents, both tough and clever, both meticulously trained. It ought to be enough. It ought to be more than enough, particularly now that one of the smugglers had been stupid enough to leave the shelter of the cavern.

He decided against the gun. Too noisy, even with the increasing whistle of the wind. He would jump the guy instead and knock him out. Sooner or later, somebody would come looking for him, and he'd get him, too.

His plans changed as someone else—no two people, three—exited the cave. Even through the fog he could see the fire of Cat's auburn hair. David Kineer was walking just in front of her. And behind her, guiding her with his hands on her upper arms, was the bearded man with the kinky hair.

There was no room inside him for hope, relief, or fear. Just concentration, nothing more. His hands were steady, his heartbeat slightly fast but even. He waited till they rounded the cliff to the cove; then he raised his gun, aiming at Kineer, and shouted, "Federal agents. Freeze!"

CHAPTER FOURTEEN

AT THE SOUND of Rob's voice the bearded smuggler flung Cat to the ground, rolled her behind a rock, and fell half on top of her. She had the presence of mind to recognize that he was defending, not attacking, her, so she didn't struggle. Still, she didn't entirely relax until she noted that his gun was pointed away from her and toward the man called Baylor. "Drop it," he ordered the confused crook as Rob leapt forward and disarmed Kineer. "I'm a friend," he told Cat as she shifted beneath his weight.

"I figured that out," she retorted. "But you're heavy nevertheless."

"Actually," said the agent as Baylor, screaming obscenities, threw down his gun, "I used to be a lot more than just a friend to you, Cat. But I suppose it's eloquent testimony to the government's plastic surgeons that you don't recognize me."

Again, that voice in the dark, considerably more nasal than she remembered, but with the same cynical inflection. And that body. You could change a face, hair, even eyes, but there wasn't much you could do about a body. "Josh?" she bit out.

"Bingo," he said, his eyes still riveted on Baylor.

Cat was surprised at the anger that ripped through her; she'd experienced more anger in one evening than she usually felt in a month. "If you don't get the hell off me, I'm going to kick you so hard you'll have to permanently alter the fit of your pants."

Josh laughed softly, but he was already moving, getting up to spread Baylor against the cliff just as Rob was doing with David. In seconds both smugglers were patted down and handcuffed while, from her corner behind the rock, Cat listened to the two undercover agents exchanging terse pleasantries. Good God! Josh, here, now. Looking like an entirely different man. They'd fixed his broken nose, altered the planes of his face, darkened his hair and permed it, reshaped his eyebrows, popped tinted contact lenses into his eyes, and . . . and what else? He'd dropped a few pounds, she thought. And grown the beard. He even walked differently.

He looked good, she conceded. But he didn't look as good as Rob.

Finally the crooks were secure, and Rob was kneeling beside her, pulling her close and touching her face with fingers that trembled. In a more tender voice than she had ever heard from him, he asked her if she was all right. She nodded. He pressed his face into her hair as he reached around and untied her wrists; she felt his lips against her scalp; she thought he murmured some sort of endearment.

Josh was giving her a funny look over Rob's head. He looked steely-eyed and sardonic. She fidgeted in Rob's arms, reminding herself that he and Josh were two of a kind.

Her lover pulled her to her feet, keeping one arm around her, holding her close against his hip. "Thank

God you thought of a way to get them out into the open," he said to Josh. "How did you know I was out here?"

"I didn't know you were out here," said Josh. He was staring at Rob's arm around Cat's waist. His lip had a subtle twist; his eyes had narrowed to slits. "It was Cat. She told us she'd seen the second boat wrecked on the rocks half a mile down the coast. You were lying, I presume, honey?"

The deliberate intimacy infuriated her, and beside her, she felt Rob stiffen. He didn't know who Josh was. Nobody did. David obviously hadn't recognized him— good heavens, poor David had been tricked twice by the same man! Despite everything, Cat felt sorry for him.

"Yes, Josh." She said his name clearly and coldly. "I was lying. If anybody'd recognize a lie when they hear one, it'd be you."

A low bank of fog drifted between them; the sea was growling, and lightning flashed high overhead. "You're Josh Evans?" Rob's arm automatically tightened around Cat's body.

"That's right." Josh's tone was less than cordial.

Rob muttered a curse. "You mean they actually put you back on this case after your cover had been blown?"

"I insisted. I had to get a new face and a complete new identity because of these bastards. I had to give up all my former connections—family, informers, *friends*"— he put subtle emphasis on the word—"because Kineer snapped a photograph of my face and splashed it across newspapers all over the country." He was speaking softly, his voice carrying only as far as Rob and Cat. "I didn't like having my life disrupted, my relationships ruined. I hated it, in fact." His eyes were very intense on Cat. "But I didn't have a helluva lot of choice at the time."

Rob knew Evans was offering Cat an apology, just as he sensed with all his masculine instincts that the other man was still attracted to the woman he loved. And Cat? He could feel her tension. She'd been crazy about this guy. She'd said it was over, that she loved *him* now, but Rob was all too cognizant of the fact that he himself had offered her nothing, made her no promises, given her no encouragement. He hadn't even told her he loved her.

Evans's words seemed to leave her cold, but how would she feel later, when the initial shock wore off? "You had a choice," she said to the man standing so stiffly opposite them. "You could have quit."

Her former lover laughed harshly. "And done what instead? There isn't much else, baby, that I'm good at."

For an instant they simply stared at one another—one woman and the two men who'd possessed her. Then Cat said tightly, "If you're so damn good at this, what about getting my grandfather and Jon out of that cave?"

"We'll get them now," said Josh. "C'mere, David, old pal." He turned and grabbed David Kineer by the collar, propelling him back in the direction of the cavern. "You're going to tell Amato to leave the hostages and get the hell out here and help salvage the wreck."

"You son of a bitch!" David screamed. "Who the hell are you anyway?"

"Your nemesis, Kineer. There'll be no suspended sentence this time. This time we're going to put you away for a nice long stretch. Let's go."

Five minutes later all three smugglers were trussed up in the cave in the place of the hostages, who were being violently hugged by Cat. Her grandfather was staring at Rob in undisguised amazement. "What's the astronomer doing with a gun in his hand?" he demanded.

Rob heard. "I'm not an astronomer; I'm a Hepburn warlord, remember?"

"He's an undercover agent," Cat explained. "He wasn't investigating UFO's; he was chasing smugglers."

"You and that other guy saved our lives," the old man grudgingly said to Rob.

"Penance, MacFarlane, for the sins of my ancestors."

* * *

Sitting on top of a box of rifles beside her grandfather, Cat watched as the two special agents—who were polite to each other but hardly warm—sorted through the contraband. She wished they'd hurry up; she wanted nothing more than to get back to her room in the castle, where she could bury her head under the covers and sob away her hurt. Josh's reappearance had shaken her profoundly, although not for the reason Rob suspected. She didn't love Josh anymore, and she no longer felt any desire for the body that, unlike the face, hadn't changed. But he was a reminder of all the things she knew and hated about the job these two men performed. A job that put weapons into their hands and gave them the power of life and death over their enemies. A job that tested them daily, driving them to the limits of their wits and strength. A job that could demand they drop family, friends, and lovers on the spur of the moment, force them to alter their names, their faces, their entire identities. She knew now why Josh had broken up with her by phone. She hadn't been allowed to see him, to know what they'd done to his face.

She remembered the mole Josh had had at the corner of his left eye. She used to love kissing that tiny imperfection. It was gone. *He* was gone. Who was he now? And, more important, who was Rob?

Actors, both of them. Chameleons. Here today and gone tomorrow. Her fists unconsciously clenched. What had possessed her to fall in love with *two* such men? Was she stupid, a masochist? Was she, like her grandfather, the sort of person who longed to see bright lights, hear sweet music—illusions that simply weren't there?

> "There once was a redheaded fool,
> Who ignored her old granddaddy's rule:
> Never fall for a man
> From the fierce Hepburn clan—
> He is ardent, but heartless and cruel."

"What did you say?" asked Rob.

"Nothing," she mumbled.

But Rob wasn't looking at her; he was watching Josh, who had apparently spoken from the mouth of the cave. "I thought I saw a light," he repeated. "Out there near the promontory."

Rob joined him at the cave entrance. "The second boat? I can't see anything. Who would try to land on a rockpile like this on such a hellish night?"

"Stupid bastards," Josh agreed. "Cat's story of a wreck'll probably come true."

Cat rose and joined them at the mouth of the cave. She, too, saw the brief flicker of a light out near the narrow entrance to the Pirates' Cove before another rush of fog obscured it. Thunder rumbled and lightning forked down, illuminating the fog soup with a strange refracted glow, and for an instant Cat thought she could see the image of a small boat.

Both men cursed. "There are explosives on that boat," Josh said. "If they hit the rocks, they might blow."

"Hell. Do you suppose they can hear our voices? The wind direction's right." Rob cupped his hands around his mouth and shouted. "You're almost on the rocks, mates! And that tub's little more than a bomb! If you've got any sense, you'll go over the side and swim for it!"

There was a faint answering shout, then silence. Cat stared out at the churning sea, the fog bank that swirled so treacherously, the potentially lethal lightning, and re-membered what Rob had said the first time they'd been together here: *I'd hate to be out there in a small boat.* Had he foreseen this? *Time doesn't exist.* Her stomach clenched as she also recalled swimming one day in a foggy lake and becoming disoriented, unable to head for shore because she didn't know where the shore was.

There was a cracking sound, a splash, and a frightened yell. Somebody called out; it sounded like a curse, then a cry of "Which way?" Good heavens! The storm was intensifying, and that water was so cold!

Rob and Josh ran out into the driving rain, yelling directions at the unfortunate sailors, but as soon as they stepped out of the cave, the wind tore the words from their mouths and scattered them in all directions. There was another loud crunch of wood; then a streak of lightning revealed the sight of a boat cracking itself against the rocks; another splash, another scream. Cat closed her eyes, horrified. Those men out there were no longer smugglers; they were people in danger of losing their lives.

Duncan MacFarlane came up behind her and laid his hands on her shoulders. "Sing, lass," her grandfather said. "Your sweet voice'll carry and give the poor sods a few moments of pleasure before they drown."

When she turned to him, shocked, she saw that his face was perfectly serious. "Might also give them the reference point they need to make the shore," he added. Then she heard another splash, from nearby this time, and Josh's "Careful, man, we don't want to lose you, too," and knew that Rob had dived into that cold, cold water to try to save the men he had been planning to arrest.

Cat opened her mouth and sang. Standing erect and breathing with every ounce of discipline she'd ever learned, she belted out her loudest, sweetest, and most alluring song, allowing the arched vault of the cavern over her head to augment its volume and waft it out over the treacherous bay. Tirelessly she sang her most poignant, powerful songs of love and loss and yearning, singing for two men she didn't know . . . and two she did: Josh Evans, who was a lost soul, and Rob Hepburn, whom she still—despite everything—longed to save. She sang while thunder crashed and rain spat; she sang while tears ran unnoticed down her cheeks. She sang as

Josh dragged two cold, scared, and half-drowned criminals out of the water, then gave a hand to their exhausted rescuer; she sang as Rob Hepburn, also cold, also dripping, but with a face that was burning with an emotion that no one, no matter how cynical or mistrustful, could look at and doubt, walked slowly up to her and said, "I love you, Siren." Then he stopped her singing with his mouth.

His kiss was an explosion of fire, bright, hot, and all-consuming. And it was echoed and reflected by the lightning that skewered out of the sky and struck the now-unoccupied smugglers' boat. There was a fire storm offshore—first the flash, then the almost deafening roar. Cursing, Rob dragged Cat back into the shelter of the cave as boom after boom exploded and hundreds of thousands of dollars worth of guns, ammunition, and God-only-knew-what-else blew heavenward. And suddenly, as if on command, the fog lifted until they could see bits of wreckage floating all over the surface of the water, burning so brightly that it seemed as if the ocean itself were aflame.

Mesmerized, everyone crowded to the mouth of the cave to watch the fire dance. Even the exhausted sailors, who had just barely escaped death, seemed awed by the water's brilliant, eerie beauty.

"Look!" said Duncan MacFarlane, his voice oddly hoarse. He was pointing inland over the promontory, some ninety degrees from the site of the explosion.

"Jeez, that's it!" Jon Hayden gasped. "Look for yourselves! I'm not drunk or crazy, after all. *That's it!*"

Still linked in each other's arms, Rob and Cat stepped out of the cave and looked up into the sky, which had turned unnaturally bright. Hovering over the cliff that hid their cave was a globelike sphere of light so bright and enormous that it dazzled both the eyes and the imagination.

"The UFO," Cat whispered.

"I don't believe it," muttered Rob. "I'm seeing it with my own eyes, and I don't believe it."

"Hush. Listen."

Then they heard an exquisite hum of sound that resembled music, although it was music of a kind that neither of them had ever heard before. It was light and liquid, a warm, sliding cascade of joyful song. And it sounded hauntingly familiar. Cat gasped as she recognized the magnificent sounds as a series of skillful variations on the melodies of her own songs.

"You called them, Siren. They're answering you."

"Oh, Rob!" Her eyes were tearing again, with joy this time. As the celestial music ended the globe burned brighter for an instant, then rotated once and streaked away, leaving behind a brief residue of light before the night sky enveloped them all in darkness once again.

Duncan MacFarlane cleared his throat. "When the waters burn, the caverns sing, and the sun showers its glory at midnight, on that fateful day shall all hatred cease and the clans be united in love," he intoned. He slapped Rob on the shoulder and shook his hand. "Looks like I have to be civil to you now, lad. The prophecy is fulfilled."

For once Rob couldn't come up with a single rational thing to say.

"Any time you want to join the Project Earth Society," MacFarlane added, his blue eyes twinkling, "we'd welcome you as a member."

Several hours later, well after dawn, Rob, on his way back to Aberdeen Castle, hurried through the woods where he and Cat had first made love. His job was done. All the smugglers had been rounded up, including the pilot, who had landed his plane just before sunup on the old airstrip, only to find himself trapped. The Agency had already flown in a contingent of men to take the criminals back to the mainland and dispose of their contraband. Josh Evans was handling the last of the mop-up operation down at Pirates' Cove.

Rob needed to talk to Cat. Now, quickly. He'd held her in his arms and shown her how he felt, but there were words, too, that needed to be said.

He'd already talked with Evans. The other man, in fact, had raised the touchy subject. "You know, don't you?" Evans had said.

"That you had something going with Cat? Yeah, I know. You hurt her badly, buddy." Rob couldn't stop the anger that had swept through him then. Nor the possessive sexual jealousy.

"I know," said Evans. "But as I told her, I didn't have a whole lot of choice."

Rob was aware from the raw note in Evans's voice that this man still had tender feelings for Cat. As Rob had guessed, Evans had apparently cared more about her than Cat had realized. "You told her you didn't love her. That you'd never loved her. That you'd just been amusing yourself."

"Yeah, well, I figured it was best to make a clean break. To take the blame all on myself. To make her hate me so she could forget me all the quicker and get on with her life." He laughed rather dryly. "Which she certainly seems to have done."

"It took her a solid year. And your damn legacy of lies and mistrust has created a wealth of obstacles for me."

"As well it should. You should be asking yourself the same questions I tormented myself with, Hepburn. You're a federal agent. What the hell have you got to offer her? Gone for weeks at a time, with no firm guarantee you'll ever make it back alive. How's she gonna live with that? She hates violence; she doesn't particularly approve of the things we have to do. Sooner or later, you'll come to the same conclusions I came to: Cat MacFarlane's too good for you, man. Just as she was too damn good for me."

"*You* might feel better if I came to those conclusions. But I'm coming to others instead. I've had all I can take of this kind of life. I'm getting the hell out."

"And doing what instead?"

Rob raised his eyes to the morning star, which was glowing faintly in the east, promising the clarity of a beautiful day after last night's violent storm. "Lucky for me, I have another profession to pursue."

There was a short silence. "You're in love with her, aren't you?" Evans said.

Rob didn't bother to confirm the obvious.

There was a longer silence this time. Finally Evans sighed and slapped Rob on the shoulder. "She's a fine lady. Be happy." Then he turned and walked away, alone.

Be happy. Rob inhaled deeply of the crisp morning air as he jogged up the hill to the castle. He intended to be.

She was waiting for him in front of the hearth in the large room where she'd been singing on the evening they'd met. Like him, she'd had no sleep all night. Like him, she was weary but wide awake. "You came back," she whispered as he walked into the room.

"Yeah. I did."

"Where's Josh?"

"He's leaving the island." He waited a moment, alert for the slightest change in her expression. There was none. "Are you sorry?"

"As far as I was concerned, Josh left the island a long, long time ago," she answered.

He stood for a moment on the threshold, relief and love pulsing so strongly in him it made him dizzy. When she touched her throat, as if searching for her grandmother's necklace, which was still in the pocket of his jeans, he finally began to move toward her. Carefully he drew it out and smiled.

"Lift your hair," he ordered when he was at her side. As she did so he slipped the fragile necklace around her neck, fastened it, then turned her in his arms. He bent his head and kissed the hollow in her throat where the heart-shaped locket lay. "I'll give you a picture of me," he said huskily. "It's going in there, with your own."

"Oh, really?" Her voice was trembling slightly. "For how long, might I ask?"

"Forever, sweetheart. I love you, Cathy." He brought his mouth to hers and drank deeply of her sweetness, feeling her love for him well up in return. "Listen. I'm quitting the Agency. I'm burned out, sick to death of it all. I want a normal life, a family, and you, Siren. You most of all."

Cat could hardly believe what she was hearing. "But, Rob—"

"Something happened to me last night," he tried to explain. "I realized that everything I've done since Beth's death has been part of a calculated attempt to give me control over my life, my fate, even death itself. I had decided I'd never be a helpless victim again, so I learned to defend myself, and others, against the most vicious sorts of criminals. And I learned other defenses, too, against emotional involvement, against love."

"Oh, Rob—"

"But I felt helpless last night, despite my gun, despite my training. I realized death is always there, always a possibility. That we are brave but fragile creatures— mortals, not gods. That you can lose someone, no matter how much you plan and scheme to prevent it. But that if you live perpetually in fear of losing, if you refuse to open up and let yourself love because the outcome might be tragic—well, I guess that's not really living at all, is it?"

"Oh, my love." Cat felt both happy and sad—a kind of pity for all he'd missed as well as an increasing spring of joy and hope for their future together. "But all this ... I understand, but it might just mean you're willing to love and need *someone* ... not necessarily me..."

He smiled tenderly. "It's you, love. I assure you, it's you I love and need. I want you to be my wife. Will you marry me?"

"You mean it, Rob, really?" She leaned her head back to look into his dark eyes. Demon eyes. Eyes you could fall into.

"I mean it," he murmured.

"Then, yes. I love you. I'd love to marry you."

He kissed her long and slow. When he raised his mouth from hers and noted the slightly quizzical look on her face, he said, "Why're you so surprised? Just because you're the first MacFarlane woman to be seduced and wed instead of seduced and abandoned?"

"Yes, as a matter of fact!"

"You see, there is such a thing as a good Hepburn."

"I never doubted it," she laughed. "But are you really going to quit your job?"

"Yup. I thought I'd take up a somewhat more sedentary profession. And atone for a few lies while I'm at it. I'm going to be an astronomer, sweetheart. And maybe investigate an unidentified flying object or two."

She grinned. "Emma's going to retire soon. Maybe you could take over her job?"

"Maybe, sweetheart. I don't care. If you want to stay on the island..."

"I do. As long as Granddad's alive." She paused, then began to laugh. "Oh, my God! Just imagine what he's going to say when he hears I'm marrying a Hepburn!"

"What he's going to say," boomed a voice from behind them, "is that it's about time you married someone, lass!"

They both turned to find Duncan MacFarlane glowering at them from the threshold. "Married, huh?" he grunted. "Well, that's all well and good, but if you don't want to feel the weight of my broadsword, lad, you'll get your lecherous hands off that woman until after your vows are said!"

"You're a surly old devil, aren't you?" Rob laughed. He pulled Cat close and kissed her lustily, exactly as he had the night they'd met.

"The wedding," her grandfather growled, "had bloody well better be soon."

CHAPTER FIFTEEN

A CASTLE, ROB Hepburn thought as he sought hand- and footholds on the rough stone wall outside Cat Mac-Farlane's bedchamber window. I don't believe I'm actually scaling the walls of a castle just for a chance to kiss my bride. Well, not *just* kiss. Gonna expect more than a kiss as a reward for this much exertion.

She was strumming her guitar and singing a haunting, unfamiliar song. Something new? Probably. Her first LP had been released to rave reviews, and her agent was after her for fresh material. She'd been working hard lately writing her music and preparing for the wedding. He'd been working hard, too, learning all the things he had to know in order to take over Emma St. Charles's job at the Aberdeen Observatory. After all, he'd been out of the field of astronomy for eight years.

Rob reached overhead for her sill and gracefully pulled himself up. Good exercise, he told himself, panting. He was going to have to find some way to keep in shape now that he wasn't running, wrestling, and shooting for a living anymore.

The window was open, thank goodness. He rested on the sill, watching her. She hadn't seen or heard him yet; she was totally involved in her music. What a beautiful voice she had, his lovely auburn-haired Siren. He watched her long, slender fingers dance over the guitar strings, her body sway gently in time to the music. His heart seemed to expand in his chest, filling him, body and soul, with love.

Pushing the window fully open, he swung one leg into the room. Cat stopped in midsong, looked, and dropped her guitar onto the bed. She was undressed for the night, clad only in a pale yellow nightgown with spaghetti straps and a neckline that revealed a good deal more than it concealed. And her grandmother's gold necklace, of course—it had his picture in it now.

She gave him a slow, infinitely sensual smile. "Hepburn devil," she said. "I thought I told you never to do that again."

"Siren," he returned, his lips caressing the word. "I heard your song and couldn't stop myself from seeking the source of such an enticing melody."

"Rob, you shouldn't be here," she protested as he angled the rest of his body through the window, dusted off his hands on his jeans, and crossed the room toward her. "It's the night before our wedding. It's bad luck or something."

"Naw. It's only bad luck for me to see you on the day of the wedding before we make it to the church. Nobody ever said anything about the *night* before."

"That's because it was assumed that the bride and groom were not in the habit of spending their nights together!"

"Well, we're not, are we? Your blasted grandfather still guards you ferociously." He came up against her, his thighs brushing hers, his hands sliding over her shoulders. "The balmy old Scot insists he doesn't want you debauched before the wedding. If he only knew!"

"Don't gloat, you lecherous wretch."

Rob slipped his hands into her hair, raising the soft, fragrant locks to his lips. "Mmm, I've missed you. If I don't get some lovin' tonight, woman, I just might not be able to control myself in church tomorrow when the minister says I'm allowed to kiss the bride."

"Now, really, not even a Hepburn would take a MacFarlane woman in the sanctuary of a church!"

Rob pushed her backward on the bed, transferred the guitar to the floor, and eased his body down on hers. "I'll take you any way I can get you, sun-child."

Cat sighed as she felt the delicious play of Rob's fingers against her bare skin. She opened her mouth under his kiss, touching tongues and shivering with the pleasure his lips and hands evoked. Impatiently she pushed at his shirt and tugged off his jeans while he lifted her night-gown and pressed kisses to her throat, her shoulders, her breasts. As always, he loved her unselfishly, spinning out the delicious preliminaries until she was more than ready for him, then entering her slowly, smoothly, and with a tender smile on his face.

As it had been from the start, the sex was dazzling, but there was more, so much more between them now. He had finally opened up to her, and what a difference it made! Now she knew him through and through—his hopes and dreams, his fears and fantasies, the things that made him happy, angry, sad.

"I love you," he whispered as he stroked her up and up to the pinnacles of earthly pleasure. "With all my heart and soul I cherish you, Cathy. Now let your body sing for me."

"Is yours singing?" she managed to ask.

"Mmm, yeah." They held each other convulsively and found release together. "I think we're in perfect harmony, Siren," he said.

* * *

"What was that song I heard as I was climbing up the wall?" he asked her a little later.

"Oh, nothing," she said too quickly.

He pushed himself up on one elbow and toyed with a burnished auburn curl. "What d'you mean, nothing? It was something new, wasn't it? I want to hear it from the beginning."

"Now?"

"Uh-huh. Now."

"It's a special song—a poem, really, that I'm setting to music. It's for tomorrow, Rob. I'm going to sing it to you in church. I wrote it for our wedding."

"You wrote a poem for our wedding?" His eyes glinted merrily at her. "Good heavens, if it's anything like the limericks you usually write for me, church is hardly the place for it! I think you'd better give me a preliminary performance right here in bed, just in case we have to censor anything."

"Don't worry, it was specially written for the wedding ceremony. I have something else planned for the wedding *night*."

"Hmm, I have a little something special planned for the wedding night myself," he said with a Groucho Marx leer.

She laughed and swatted him playfully. "You would!"

He reached for her guitar. "Come on, sweetheart, sing."

"Okay. I hope you like it." She took the guitar, pushed herself back against the headboard, and covered herself decorously with the sheet. Smiling at him, she struck several gentle chords. "It's called 'Celebration,' and it's in honor of our marriage and our love." And she began:

"Love me with the devotion of the wolf,
    Who finds his mate and stays forever true,
    And with the joy of moondance on the deep;

Melt me with the dragon's golden heat,
Spin laughter like a flashing coin,
And comfort me in grief;
Hold me steadfast as the mariner,
Who dares the angered sea;
Love me with the tolerance of God.

"Come, soul-friend, take my hand,
It is our wedding feast,
Our separate journeys now are one."

When she finished, Rob's dark demon eyes were heavy-lidded with emotion. "That's beautiful, Cathy," he whispered. "Is that really how you feel about me?"

She put the guitar down and opened her arms for him. "Don't you know by now how I feel about you, you silly man? I know, finally, how you feel about *me.*"

"But I can't put it into words. Not like that, anyway." He kissed her lovingly. "I wish I could. You give me so much. I wish I had a similar gift for you. Something creative, something I could make for you that would always be an expression of my love."

She grinned a little mischievously. "Actually, there is something you could give me that would be creative . . . a permanent expression of our love."

"There is? What?"

"A child, Rob. Would you like to have a baby?"

"Oh, love, you know I want a child. Any time. As soon as you're ready. As soon as—"

"How about nine months from tonight?"

"What do you mean?"

"I mean you just invaded my bedchamber unexpectedly, giving me no opportunity to take any precautions, and it's my fertile time of the month."

"Oh, jeez! You think you're pregnant already?"

She was tilting her head to one side, as if listening to her body. "I don't know . . . I couldn't possibly know yet,

of course, but I just have this feeling . . . a sort of intuition
. . . it's not rational at all, but—"

"To hell with rational. After witnessing the Siren lure
sailors out of the sea, watching an ancient prophecy come
true before my eyes, and having a close encounter with
an actual UFO, I'm a convert to the world of mystery
and illusion. If you have a feeling you're pregnant, you
probably are. Good God, this'll be a shotgun wedding,
after all. Your grandfather will kill me!"

"What's one night?" she laughed. "He'll never know."

He slid down in bed and pressed a kiss to her silken
smooth belly. "Just think," he whispered against her skin,
"maybe there's a lusty redheaded lad developing in there,
with a combined talent for poetry and wall-climbing."

"Or a dark-haired daughter who can sing like a Siren
and shoot a gun like Annie Oakley."

His gentle caresses lingered, and lingered . . . until
gradually she began to breathe more quickly and shift
her limbs restlessly. "Rob?"

"Uh-huh, sun-child?"

"I could be wrong. I might not be pregnant yet. But
I'd like to be."

He chuckled. "In which case we should try a little
harder?"

"Well, yes, to, uh, increase the odds. I know it hasn't
been very long, but do you suppose you could . . ."

He raised himself on his forearms and moved against
her, proving instantly that he not only *could* but was
going to. "When I first saw you, you know the ridiculous
idea that ran through my head?" he asked huskily as he
gently parted her thighs.

"What?" she choked out.

"I had this totally irrational feeling that you were
destined to be my love."

"Very silly."

"An illusion," he agreed. He moved, filling her deliciously. "What you were really destined to be was my wife and the mother of my children."

"Oh, yes," she murmured, matching her rhythm with his.

"And you know what else I've decided?" he persisted as she tossed her head from side to side on the pillow.

"What else have you ... oh, Rob ... I don't think I can talk anymore."

He sounded a little incoherent himself. "That time doesn't exist ... that we've lived before and will live again ... that our souls have known and loved each other many times and will be together always."

"Oh, Rob, I think you're right."

"I know I'm right, sun-child."

"Listen," she said a few moments later as sweet relief came to both of them. "Do you hear something, or is it my imagination?"

Rob listened, then looked toward the open window, where, for an instant, he thought he caught a glimpse of a dazzling globe of light. It seemed to be showering heavenly music upon him and his beloved. He heard it ... or was it only the pounding rhythms of their hearts? He shook his head slowly. "I don't know, love. But as long as we believe it's there and that it's giving us its blessing, who cares?"

Cat sighed and nestled close. "Come, soul-friend, take my hand," she murmured, pressing her palm into his.

His fingers closed over hers. "Our separate journeys now are one."

Second Chance at Love ®

___ 0-425-08200-8	LOVE PLAY #269 Carole Buck	$2.25
___ 0-425-08201-6	CAN'T SAY NO #270 Jeanne Grant	$2.25
___ 0-425-08202-4	A LITTLE NIGHT MUSIC #271 Lee Williams	$2.25
___ 0-425-08203-2	A BIT OF DARING #272 Mary Haskell	$2.25
___ 0-425-08204-0	THIEF OF HEARTS #273 Jan Mathews	$2.25
___ 0-425-08284-9	MASTER TOUCH #274 Jasmine Craig	$2.25
___ 0-425-08285-7	NIGHT OF A THOUSAND STARS #275 Petra Diamond	$2.25
___ 0-425-08286-5	UNDERCOVER KISSES #276 Laine Allen	$2.25
___ 0-425-08287-3	MAN TROUBLE #277 Elizabeth Henry	$2.25
___ 0-425-08288-1	SUDDENLY THAT SUMMER #278 Jennifer Rose	$2.25
___ 0-425-08289-X	SWEET ENCHANTMENT #279 Diana Mars	$2.25
___ 0-425-08461-2	SUCH ROUGH SPLENDOR #280 Cinda Richards	$2.25
___ 0-425-08462-0	WINDFLAME #281 Sarah Crewe	$2.25
___ 0-425-08463-9	STORM AND STARLIGHT #282 Lauren Fox	$2.25
___ 0-425-08464-7	HEART OF THE HUNTER #283 Liz Grady	$2.25
___ 0-425-08465-5	LUCKY'S WOMAN #284 Delaney Devers	$2.25
___ 0-425-08466-3	PORTRAIT OF A LADY #285 Elizabeth N. Kary	$2.25
___ 0-425-08508-2	ANYTHING GOES #286 Diana Morgan	$2.25
___ 0-425-08509-0	SOPHISTICATED LADY #287 Elissa Curry	$2.25
___ 0-425-08510-4	THE PHOENIX HEART #288 Betsy Osborne	$2.25
___ 0-425-08511-2	FALLEN ANGEL #289 Carole Buck	$2.25
___ 0-425-08512-0	THE SWEETHEART TRUST #290 Hilary Cole	$2.25
___ 0-425-08513-9	DEAR HEART #291 Lee Williams	$2.25
___ 0-425-08514-7	SUNLIGHT AND SILVER #292 Kelly Adams	$2.25
___ 0-425-08515-5	PINK SATIN #293 Jeanne Grant	$2.25
___ 0-425-08516-3	FORBIDDEN DREAM #294 Karen Keast	$2.25
___ 0-425-08517-1	LOVE WITH A PROPER STRANGER #295 Christa Merlin	$2.25
___ 0-425-08518-X	FORTUNE'S DARLING #296 Frances Davies	$2.25
___ 0-425-08519-8	LUCKY IN LOVE #297 Jacqueline Topaz	$2.25
___ 0-425-08626-7	HEARTS ARE WILD #298 Janet Gray	$2.25
___ 0-425-08627-5	SPRING MADNESS #299 Aimée Duvall	$2.25
___ 0-425-08628-3	SIREN'S SONG #300 Linda Barlow	$2.25
___ 0-425-08629-1	MAN OF HER DREAMS #301 Katherine Granger	$2.25
___ 0-425-08630-5	UNSPOKEN LONGINGS #302 Dana Daniels	$2.25
___ 0-425-08631-3	THIS SHINING HOUR #303 Antonia Tyler	$2.25

Prices may be slightly higher in Canada.

QUESTIONNAIRE

1. How do you rate _____
                              (please print TITLE)
   - ☐ excellent   ☐ good
   - ☐ very good   ☐ fair   ☐ poor

2. How likely are you to purchase another book in this series?
   - ☐ definitely would purchase
   - ☐ probably would purchase
   - ☐ probably would not purchase
   - ☐ definitely would not purchase

3. How likely are you to purchase another book by this author?
   - ☐ definitely would purchase
   - ☐ probably would purchase
   - ☐ probably would not purchase
   - ☐ definitely would not purchase

4. How does this book compare to books in other contemporary romance lines?
   - ☐ much better
   - ☐ better
   - ☐ about the same
   - ☐ not as good
   - ☐ definitely not as good

5. Why did you buy this book? (Check as many as apply)
   - ☐ I have read other SECOND CHANCE AT LOVE romances
   - ☐ friend's recommendation
   - ☐ bookseller's recommendation
   - ☐ art on the front cover
   - ☐ description of the plot on the back cover
   - ☐ book review I read
   - ☐ other _____
     _____
     _____

(Continued...)

6. Please list your three favorite contemporary romance lines.

_____
_____

7. Please list your favorite authors of contemporary romance lines.

_____
_____
_____
_____
_____
_____

8. How many SECOND CHANCE AT LOVE romances have you read? _____

9. How many series romances like SECOND CHANCE AT LOVE do you <u>read</u> each month? _____

10. How many series romances like SECOND CHANCE AT LOVE do you <u>buy</u> each month? _____

11. Mind telling your age?
       ☐ under 18
       ☐ 18 to 30
       ☐ 31 to 45
       ☐ over 45

☐ Please check if you'd like to receive our <u>free</u> SECOND CHANCE AT LOVE Newsletter.

We hope you'll share your other ideas about romances with us on an additional sheet and attach it securely to this questionnaire.

• •

Fill in your name and address below:
Name _____
Street Address _____
City _____ State _____ Zip _____

Please return this questionnaire to:
  SECOND CHANCE AT LOVE
  The Berkley Publishing Group
  200 Madison Avenue, New York, New York 10016